THE STORY OF YOUNG MINDS

A VOYAGE THROUGH TIME & SPACE

SUMIT KUMAR

INDIA • SINGAPORE • MALAYSIA

ISBN 979-8-89026-961-4

Dedication

I would like to dedicate this book to the young authors of the stories in this book, whose creativity and passion have made this project possible.

Additionally, I would like to express my gratitude to my parents, friends, brother, sister, wife, daughter, and the entire Team Velocity for their unwavering support and encouragement throughout this journey.

I would also like to extend my heartfelt gratitude to my science teacher, Shri Ram Suchit Vishwakarma, whose guidance and mentorship have been instrumental in shaping my curiosity and interest in the world of science.

CONTENTS

एन एम देसाई / N M Desai
विशिष्ट वैज्ञानिक / Distinguished Scientist
निदेशक / Director

भारत सरकार GOVERNMENT OF INDIA
अंतरिक्ष विभाग DEPARTMENT OF SPACE
अंतरिक्ष उपयोग केंद्र
SPACE APPLICATIONS CENTRE
अहमदाबाद AHMEDABAD - 380015
(भारत) / (INDIA)
दूरभाष / PHONE:+91-79-26913344, 26928401
फैक्स / FAX : +91-79-26915843
ई-मेल / E-mail: director@sac.isro.gov.in

FOREWORD

I am honored to write the foreword for 'The Story of Young Minds,' a unique and brilliant collection of science fiction stories written by school children, with passion for space science and talent for weaving captivating science fiction tales. Science fiction has always been a great source of inspiration, and it is wonderful to see such young minds exploring this genre and contributing in their unique ways.

It is also heartening to note that these ***young minds have been given the opportunity to show case their creativity through a "Science Fiction Story Writing Competition" organized by Team Velocity, formed by my SAC/ISRO colleague, Mr. Sumit Kumar.*** His dedication and pursuit of encouraging young minds shines through the pages of this book. The book in itself is a testament to the power of creative expression and the limitless potential of the human imagination that lies within each and every child.

I am sure this, is the book that will inspire and delight readers of all ages, and will be a tribute to the visionary work of Mr. Sumit Kumar and his team in shaping the minds and futures of Generation Z. As ***I turned the pages of 'The Story of Young Minds,'*** I felt that I was ***transported to a world beyond my imagination.*** Each story in this book takes us on a journey through the universe, exploring new worlds, encountering strange creatures, and facing daunting challenges. As I read on, I couldn't help but ***feel a sense of wonder and excitement. These young writers have truly captured the essence of space science in their stories.*** Through their work, they have ***demonstrated that science fiction is not just about predicting the future but also about inspiring curiosity and wonder*** about the world around us. They have imagined new worlds and new technologies and have shown us the potential that these advancements have to change our lives for the better.

SAC and ISRO have always encouraged young people to explore their interests in science and technology. It is through this exploration that we can find solutions to some of the most pressing and complex challenges facing mother Earth today. By fostering the curiosity and creativity of young minds, we can ensure that the future of science and technology lie in capable and talented hands.

I believe that this collection of stories is not only an inspiration to young readers but also a testimony to the power of the human imagination. ***I compliment and congratulate the young authors, who contributed***

towards this book, for their hard work and dedication and also offer my sincere gratitude to their teachers and mentors, who have encouraged them along the way. May many such endeavors galore!

(एन एम देसाई / (N M Desai)
निदेशक / Director

FOREWORD

Dr. Vikram Sarabhai dreamt of having a rocket of our own technology for India and once said, **"He who can listen to the music in the midst of noise can achieve great things."** Mr. Sumit Kumar listened to the music of creativity and ignited the minds of children by introducing them to rocket science. He traveled from school to school, imparting knowledge about rocket science through lectures and showcasing rocket models. Sumit has always harbored a love for adventure, which he has been fortunate enough to share with his family and friends. The novel idea he conceived to spread the science of rockets among children was to solicit their views through science fiction story writing competitions. The compilation of thirty stories in the book titled "The Story of Young Minds," part of the Amazing Science Fiction series, showcases the children's imagination as they write captivating stories about spacecraft, planets, and the vastness of space.

"The Story of Young Minds" offers a captivating array of science fiction stories, each presenting unique and imaginative narratives. It captivates readers with an array of thought-provoking science fiction stories that tackle various themes and concepts. With each unique story, "The Story of Young Minds" offer readers an enthralling collection of science fiction narratives that spark the imagination and transport them to extraordinary realms. From the quest for water on Mars to interplanetary journeys and mind-bending cosmic phenomena, this book promises an exhilarating reading experience for science fiction enthusiasts of all ages.

With each story, "The Story of Young Minds" sparks curiosity, imagination, and a sense of wonder. From environmental consciousness to space exploration, these narratives offer an engaging and inspiring reading experience that will transport readers to worlds both familiar and beyond. The stories in the book truly showcase the creative prowess and boundless imagination of its young authors. With tales of time machines, space wars, genetic breakthroughs, and encounters with otherworldly beings, this collection promises a riveting reading experience that will leave readers eager for more.

This book is not only inspiring for young readers but also a true testament to the incredible power of imagination. I want to commend the young authors who worked hard and dedicated themselves to create these stories. I also want to congratulate the Team Velocity for supporting and guiding them along the way.

Together, they have brought forth a remarkable book that showcases the limitless possibilities of storytelling and the incredible talent of these young minds.

Vinod Kumar Srivastava
Former Scientist,
Satish Dhawan Space Center,
Indian Space Research Organisation,
Sriharikota, Andhra Pradesh

MUST READ, WHAT THESE SCIENTISTS SAY ABOUT THE STORIES, WHICH WILL MAKE YOU CURIOUS TO READ THIS BOOK!!

WHAT THESE SCIENTISTS SAY...

Mr. Sumit Kumar has always been involved in educational activities to inspire and motivate students by sharing his knowledge about space science. "The Story of Young Minds" is a testament to Mr. Kumar's dedication to education and his ability to inspire creativity and imagination in others. I highly recommend this book to anyone who loves science fiction and is looking for an inspiring read that will transport them to new worlds and beyond.

Jitendra Kumar Sharma, Scientist, ISRO

"The Story of Young Minds" is more than just a collection of stories. It is a testament to the power of education, guidance, and the unwavering belief in the creative potential of young minds. Mr. Kumar's dedication to inspiring and motivating students is evident in the quality of the narratives presented in the book. From tales of interstellar travel to mind-bending journeys through time and space, each story offers a unique perspective on the mysteries of the universe.

Akhilesh Sharma, Scientist, ISRO

Each story in the book - "The Story of Young Minds" offers a unique perspective on the mysteries of the universe, ranging from intergalactic adventures to mind-bending time travel. Some stories focus on the power of technology and the consequences of playing with time and space, while others explore the importance of human connections and the bonds that transcend even the most extraordinary circumstances. "The Story of Young Minds" is a must-read for anyone who loves science fiction.

Dr. Hemant Arora, Scientist, ISRO

"The Story of Young Minds" is an amazing book filled with science fiction stories written by the young authors, who have shown incredible creativity and imagination beyond their years and taking us on thrilling journeys through space and time. I want to give a big shout-out to the author, Sumit Kumar, for his remarkable efforts in inspiring and nurturing these young minds. I highly recommend "The Story of Young Minds" to everyone seeking an inspiring and enjoyable read.

Jitendra Kumar Pandey, Scientist, BARC

Featuring tales from budding young writers, this book takes readers on a journey through the cosmos and beyond. From interstellar adventures to mind-bending time travel, each story in the book offers a unique perspective on the mysteries of the universe. Discover new worlds and witness the incredible power of science and technology as you delve into these gripping tales of exploration and discovery. I highly recommended the book - "The Story of Young Minds" for science fiction lovers.

Arpita Gajaria Bhatia, Scientist, ISRO

"The Story of Young Minds" is a captivating collection of science fiction stories written by school students. Despite their young age, the authors showcase an impressive level of creativity and imagination, taking readers on a journey through the vast expanse of space and time. "The Story of Young Minds" is highly recommended for fans of science fiction and anyone looking to be inspired by the next generation of great writers.

Ravi Kumar Varma, Scientist, ISRO

"The Story of Young Minds" is a wonderful book that showcases the remarkable imagination and creativity of young authors under the guidance of Mr. Sumit Kumar and his Team Velocity. This collection of science fiction stories takes readers on thrilling journeys through space, time, and beyond. The young writers explore the mysteries of the universe and share their unique perspectives, creating a truly inspiring read.

Anil Sukheja, Scientist, ISRO

"The Story of Young Minds" is a thrilling collection of science fiction stories that explore the vast unknowns of space and time. This book is a testament to the boundless imagination and creativity of the next generation of science fiction writers. So, if you're looking for a thrilling journey through the depths of space and time, look no further than "The Story of Young Minds."

Hiren Arvind Rambhia, Scientist, ISRO

ACKNOWLEDGMENTS

Writing a book is a journey, and it's one that I could not have taken alone. I owe a debt of gratitude to many people who have contributed to this project in countless ways.

First and foremost, I would like to thank my family for their unwavering support and encouragement. Their love and patience sustained me through the long hours and many rewrites that went into this book.

I also owe a huge debt of thanks to my friends, who tirelessly worked with me to shape and refine the manuscript. Their insights and editorial guidance were invaluable, and I am grateful for their belief in this project.

To my colleagues and friends who read early drafts of the manuscript and offered feedback, I am indebted to your honesty and insight. Your feedback helped me to shape and refine the book, and I could not have done it without you.

Finally, I would like to express my appreciation to the readers who will ultimately read this book. Your interest and support mean the world to me, and I hope that this work will in some small way enrich your life.

Thank you to all who have helped me on this journey. I am deeply grateful for your support and encouragement.

PREFACE

The world of science fiction has always been a fascinating realm for exploring new ideas, pushing boundaries, and imagining what could be possible. As a scientist, I have been fortunate enough to witness the power of this genre in inspiring creativity and fostering imagination in my young authors.

This book is a collection of science fiction stories written by the young minds, ranging from middle school to high school age. These young writers have taken the concepts and themes of science fiction and transformed them into their own unique visions, crafting stories that are both entertaining and thought-provoking.

The stories in this book showcase the incredible talent, creativity, and potential of young writers. Each story is a testament to the power of imagination, and a reminder that the future is in the hands of the next generation.

While the stories in this book vary in their style, setting, and subject matter, they all share a common thread of curiosity and wonder. They challenge us to think beyond what we know, to imagine a world where anything is possible, and to confront the potential consequences of the choices we make.

I hope that this collection of stories will inspire others to explore the world of science fiction, to embrace their own creativity, and to never stop asking **"what if? "**.

Thank you to all the young authors who contributed to this book, and to their families, teachers, and mentors who have supported them along the way. It has been a pleasure to guide these young writers on their creative journey, and I am excited to share their work with the world.

Sincerely,
[Sumit Kumar]

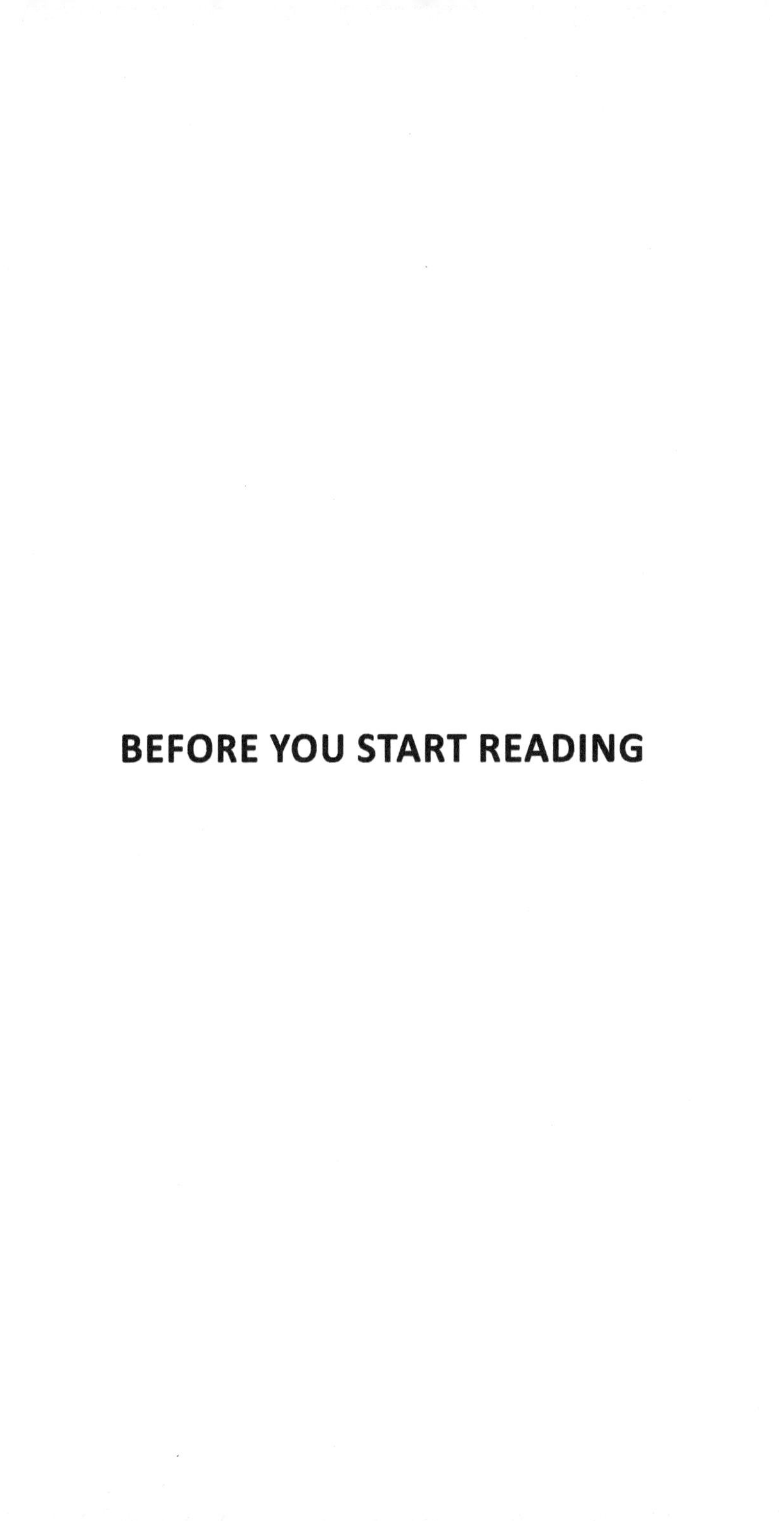

BEFORE YOU START READING

TEAM VELOCITY

Team Velocity is a dedicated group of experienced individuals hailing from diverse backgrounds, including education, arts, science, and technology. Our core objective is to enrich the knowledge and education of poor children across the nation. As part of our efforts, we conduct national-level events and competitions specifically targeted towards school children, aimed at promoting and popularizing education among them.

Our focus lies primarily in the rural areas of our country, where education and awareness about its importance are often lacking. By conducting these events and competitions, we aim to spread awareness about education and encourage children to take an active interest in their studies.

The driving force behind our vision is to reach every underprivileged child in the country and inspire them to pursue education. We firmly believe that every child has the right to quality education and our team is committed to making that a reality. Through our collective efforts, we strive to make a positive impact on the lives of these children and contribute towards a brighter future for them and the country as a whole.

MEMBERS OF TEAM VELOCITY

Sumit Kumar hails from a small town of Khaga-Fatehpur, Uttar Pradesh. He studied electronics and communication engineering from Dr. A.P.J. Abdul Kalam Technical University (earlier UPTU), Lucknow, and working as a scientist in ISRO, Ahmedabad, Gujarat. He enjoys writing, travelling, reading, and watching movies.

Sushil Kumar belongs to Saharanpur, Uttar Pradesh. He has done his B.Tech. from Dr. A.P.J. Abdul Kalam Technical University (earlier UPTU) and M. Tech. from MDU University, Rohtak. He is working in Union Bank of India, Saharanpur. Formally he worked as an assistant professor in Al-Falah School of Engineering and Technology. He likes reading scientific generals, watching movies, traveling.

Ravinder Kumar belongs to Saharanpur, Uttar Pradesh. He has done his B.Tech from Dr. A.P.J. Abdul Kalam Technical University (earlier UPTU). He is currently working in an MNC, New- Delhi. He likes reading books, watching movies, traveling.

Ashutosh Prajapati belongs to Lucknow, Uttar Pradesh. He has done his B.Tech in Mechanical Engineering from Rajeev Gandhi Technical University, Bhopal. Currently he is working in Sensors and Measurements Private Ltd., Lucknow. He likes travelling, exploring new places, watching movies and listening songs.

Vivek Kumar belongs to Barabanki, Uttar Pradesh. He has done his B. Tech from Dr. A.P.J. Abdul Kalam Technical University (earlier UPTU) and working as a scientist in ISRO, Ahmedabad, and Gujarat. He enjoys playing and watching cricket.

Heena Setia hails from Hisar, Haryana and has obtained her B.Tech degree from Maharishi Dayanand University located in Rohtak, Haryana. She has over seven years of experience working as a scientist with ISRO. Currently, she is pursuing her Master's degree at the University of Southern California in the United States. In her free time, she enjoys reading, watching movies, and traveling.

M. Mahendhiran belongs to Villupuram district, Tamilnadu. He is currently working as scientific assistant at ISRO. He studied M.Sc Animation and vfx since been involved in various projects related to design, Animation and visualisation. He enjoys cycling, playing video games.

Anand Mohan Roy hails from Bhagalpur district of Bihar. He has studied his B. Tech. in Electronics and Communication Engineering from Sardar Vallabh Bhai National Institute of Technology, Surat and currently working as a scientist in ISRO, Ahmedabad, and Gujarat.. He enjoys travelling, singing and listening music.

Hima Medapareddy belongs to Visakhapatnam, Andhra Pradesh. She did her bachelor's degree in Avionics from the prestigious Indian Institute of Space Science and Technology (IIST). She is currently working as Scientist in ISRO. She has a passion for sports and loves to stay active and engaged in physical activities. She is known for exceptional event organizing skills, having successfully planned and executed numerous events in her career. Additionally, She enjoys participating in outreach programs for various events and occasions.

Neelkamal Singh currently lives in Bangalore, Karnataka. He has done is B.Sc (Computer Science) from Andhra University and M.Sc (Computer Science) from Annamalai University. He is working as Assistant Manager in Eli Lilly US Pharmaceutical firm. Formally he was founder of LetMeSpark Services. His hobbies includes travelling, reading novels, cooking and watching movies.

Archana Rajput belongs to Mainpuri, Uttar- Pradesh. She has completed her B.Tech from Kamla Nehru Institute of Technology, Sultanpur, Uttar Pradesh. She is working as a primary teacher in Kendriya Vidyalaya Sangathan under Ministry of Education and currently posted at KV Viramgam Ahmedabad Gujarat. She likes paintings, art-works and craft works. She love to spend time with poor kids, like to listen their stories and experiences of life.

Kavita Singh belongs to Prayagraj, Uttar Pradesh. She has completed her B.Com. in Information System and Management from GSS Jain College, University of Madras. She is currently working as project manager in Tata Communications, Chennai, TamilNadu. She love reading novels, exploring new places and food.

Objective of Team Velocity:

The primary objective of Team Velocity is to enable the youth of the country to become self-sufficient through education and technical knowledge. To achieve this, we adopt an innovative and entrepreneurial approach in various fields. Our goal is to empower people in different regions of the country through education, enabling them to play an active role in the development of the country.

We believe that education is a powerful tool for transforming the lives of individuals, families, and communities. Through our initiatives, we strive to provide access to quality education to individuals from all walks of life. By promoting education and technical knowledge, we aim to equip people with the education tool they need to become self-reliant and contribute positively towards the growth and development of the country.

Our team's ultimate aim is to create a self-sustaining ecosystem that encourages innovation, creativity, and entrepreneurship among the youth. We are committed to working towards this goal and making a positive impact on the lives of the poor people.

"If a story is in you, it has to come out"

– William Faulkner,

American writer & noble laureate

Let's dive into the world of imagination!

This is a world where anything is possible and the only limit is our own creativity. With imagination, we can create entire universes, travel through time and space, and bring to life characters and creatures that only exist in our minds. It's a world that's free from the constraints of reality and allows us to explore the depths of our own inner worlds. So let's take the plunge and see where our imaginations can take us!

in search of
water
WRITTEN BY
AKHIL SHARMA
REG. NO., VSFSWC-20220073
Class - 8
School - Euro International School
Gurgaon, Haryana
© Team Velocity

1

IN SEARCH OF WATER

"If there is magic on this planet, it is contained in water."

– Loren Eiseley

After the successful establishment of the first human colony on the planet Mars, the people living there on the red planet called "Marstronauts" sought to discover a large water source on the planet. The only two known sources of water were frozen ice caps situated at the northern and southern poles of the planet. The Marstronauts, comprised of members from various space agencies including NASA, ISRO, and SpaceX, embarked on a joint mission to reach the northern ice cap to conduct tests on the frozen water to determine its safety for consumption. To accomplish this task, they needed to select a highly experienced and courageous astronaut to travel in a specialized vehicle to the ice cap, collect samples of the frozen water, and return safely to the Mars Base. This mission required a great deal of bravery, courage, and boldness.

"Attention Marstronauts! We are having a special meeting in the main hall. Please make your way there as quickly as possible." The announcer's voice boomed through the sleep room, rousing all the Marstronauts from their slumber. They hastily donned their spacesuits and made their way to the main hall.

"Good morning, Marstronauts!" greeted the Colonel, the head of the team.

"Good morning, sir!" the crew responded in unison.

"As you all know, we are in desperate need of search a substantial water source, as our current supply from the Earth is running low." the Colonel continued. "Therefore, we have decided to launch a one-man expedition this afternoon, and the selected candidate is Alfredo."

There was an audible gasp from the assembled Marstronauts. They had expected the Colonel to choose a brave and fearless explorer for such a critical mission, but Alfredo was neither. He was known to be timid and fearful, even scared of venturing into a different room alone.

"So, Alfredo, I request that you come with me to see your vehicle," said the Colonel, leading Alfredo to another compartment as the other Marstronauts left the main hall.

When the Colonel's assistant removed the cover from the vehicle, Alfredo was amazed.

"Allow me to introduce Carlos 368-B!" declared the Colonel, "The fastest hovering vehicle, equipped with self-driving technology, wireless communication systems, soothing music, and comfortable seating." The vehicle's designer, a professor, chimed in, "But that's not all!"

"Sir, this is all very impressive, but why was I chosen for this mission?" asked Alfredo.

The Colonel's assistant responded, "Sorry, that information is classified, Sir."

The Colonel replied, "We'll explain everything upon your return, Alfredo. You have 60 minutes to prepare before departing."

"After getting ready, Alfredo proceeded to the departure center where the Colonel awaited him.

"Are you ready to go?" the Colonel asked.

"Yes, sir," replied Alfredo.

"The journey to the Northern Ice Cap should take around 6.5 hours. I've already programmed the directions into Carlos, so it will navigate autonomously," added the assistant.

With a farewell, Alfredo boarded Carlos and initiated the hovercraft. In no time, they reached a desert-like region, leaving behind the last of the Mars Base buildings.

"It's not bad. It's like driving a car on Earth, but I'm concerned about going alone," Alfredo murmured to himself.

Later, he fell asleep, only to awaken to the realization that he was just 2 hours and 52 minutes away from the Ice Cap. He then contacted the Mars Base via communication device, and a fellow Marstronaut answered the call. "Hello?" they said.

"Hi, this is Alfredo, Marstronaut No. 73. Can you connect me with the Colonel, please?"

"Sure, just a moment," they responded. "

"Hello, Alfredo! This is Colonel. How is the journey going?" The Colonel's voice trailed off as the signal cut out, and Carlos came to an abrupt halt. A red light flashed on the screen, reading 'Emergency Shut Down!'.

Alfredo felt his fear rising. Despite multiple attempts, he could not establish contact with the Mars Base. Nothing except the oxygen supply was functional in the Carlos hovercraft. The Carlos had been caught in a Mars sandstorm, causing the engine to fail.

However, Alfredo remained resolute in his determination to investigate the Polar Ice Cap for usable water. Equipping himself with a spacesuit, 10 hours of oxygen, and necessary gear and testing machine, Alfredo checked the map of the planet Mars on his mini-communication device and stepped out of the Carlos to confront the storm. Though the wind was fierce, Alfredo's spacesuit protected him, and he shut the door of the Carlos before setting out on foot towards the Ice Cap, guided by the mini-GPS on his spacesuit.

As the sun set and darkness fell, he marched ahead. The mini-GPS showed that it would take 4 hours and 6 minutes to reach the Ice Cap by foot, while the Carlos could have covered the same distance in just 2 hours and 50 minutes!"

Despite the challenges, Alfredo remained determined. After walking for 3 hours straight, he took a 5-minute break and attempted to contact the Mars Base. The sky had cleared up and the sandstorm had dissipated. Suddenly, a voice came through on Alfredo's communication device: "Hello? Alfredo, this is Colonel. Where are you right now? We lost communication with Carlos and thought we might have lost you as well."

"I have been walking continuously towards the Polar Ice Cap for the past 3 hours," Alfredo responded.

"According to my Mini-GPS, it will take approximately one more hour to get there."

"Alfredo, it's night time and not safe to travel alone," the Colonel advised. "I'm sending a rescue team to your location. Just send me your coordinates."

"I appreciate your concern, Sir," Alfredo replied, "but I am committed to completing this mission no matter what. I will see it through to the end."

"Are you absolutely sure about this, Alfredo?" the Colonel asked.

"Yes, Sir, I am sure," Alfredo replied resolutely.

Alfredo hung up the call and continued walking towards the polar ice cap. After half an hour, he became thirsty also but finally he reached the ice cap. He touched the frozen ice and inserted the testing machine, but all he could see was ice everywhere. Overwhelmed by exhaustion, Alfredo fainted.

When he regained consciousness, he found himself in the medical center of his Mars Base. The Colonel, Professor, and Assistant were there to see him.

"How did I get back here, Sir?" Alfredo asked.

"Don't worry about it. When you fainted at the Polar Ice Cap, the testing machine switched on and gave us your location. We were able to find you with the help of that information. Our rescue team brought you back here, along with the testing machine," explained the Colonel.

Alfredo then asked, "What were the results of the testing machine?"

The Colonel replied, "It worked. We can use the water from the frozen ice cap. Our mission is a success!"

"And sir, I'm curious about one last thing. You said earlier that you would tell me why you chose me for this mission. So sir, why did you choose me?" asked Alfredo.

"Well, it's simple," replied the Colonel. "If we had chosen a Marstronaut who relied solely on their intellect, they may have made the logical decision to turn back during an emergency, like the one you faced. However, we knew that you would follow your heart, even in the face of adversity, and that made you the most dedicated and committed candidate for this mission."

***

"Thousands have lived without love, not one without water."

– W. H. Auden

WRITTEN BY
SHREENITHI
SENTHIL

CLASS - 7
VELAMMAL VIDHYASHRAM, SURAPET
CHENNAI, TAMIL NADU

REG. NO.- VSFSWC-202220179

2

THE ADVENTURE OF PETER

"There is no certainty; there is only adventure."

– Roberto Assagioli

Once, there was a happy family of four consisting of Diana, the mother, Edward Joseph, the father, and their two children - a boy named Peter and his sister, Alice.

Edward Joseph, Peter and Alice's father, worked as an accountant in a large firm in the city. He was a hardworking man who spent long hours at the office, but he always made time for his family whenever he could. Diana, Peter and Alice's mother, was a homemaker who dedicated her time to taking care of her family and their home. She was a loving and nurturing mother who made sure that her children were always well-fed, clothed, and happy. Diana enjoyed cooking and baking, and she often prepared delicious meals and treats for her family to enjoy.

Peter was a smart and active young boy who loved sports and outdoor activities. He was the eldest child in the family, and he always looked out for his younger sister Alice. Peter was also an avid reader and had a curious mind, always asking questions and seeking new knowledge. In his free time, Peter enjoyed playing football, basketball, and baseball, and he was always eager to join a game with his friends. He was also interested in science and loved conducting experiments and learning about how things work. Peter had a kind heart and was always ready to help others in need.

Peter and Alice were proud of their parents and appreciated all that they did for them. They knew that their father worked hard to provide for their family, and they admired their mother for her loving care and dedication to their home. Despite their different roles, both parents were equally important in their family, and Peter and Alice felt grateful to have them in their lives.

However, their happiness was short-lived as Edward's mother fell ill and was on her deathbed. To visit her at her home, Peter's parents packed for their travel needs and decided to leave the children behind, with Peter being the only one responsible for his younger sister. Despite their desire to accompany their parents, they were good students who did not want to miss their classes.

When their parents left, Peter went for a walk and stumbled upon a new creature he had never seen before. Being the curious boy he is, he tried to chase and catch it, but it kept evading him. After a long pursuit, he finally caught it and took it back to their house, where he narrated the incident to his sister. Intrigued by the mysterious creature, they searched for it on the internet but found nothing about the mysterious creature. As the creature seemed harmless, they decided to keep it as a pet. Although it was quite late, they went to study as they were both interested in their studies.

Today was Sunday, and Peter had to submit his weekly project the next day. He wanted to make a mini rocket to show in his class, but it took him a lot of time to build it, with many complicated and fancy calculations. To their surprise, the pet was very clever and helped Peter with his calculations. He successfully completed his mini rocket and went to sleep happily.

On the contrary, Alice was struggling with her Math's assignment and had an exam scheduled for the next day. Usually, she relied on her brother or mother to assist her with Math's. However, her mother was out, and her brother was preoccupied with his project. This left Alice grappling with all the problems by herself. She spent nearly two hours on a single problem, feeling stuck and helpless. Frustrated, she wandered into her brother's room, where she noticed her pet attempting to communicate with her. Upon approaching the pet, it swiftly solved the problem, returned the book to her, and they proceeded to tackle the Math's assignment together.

It was also a great playmate. The siblings named it Berry, which meant "joy of the world" in their language, and Berry was pleased with its name. After playing for some time, they eventually fell asleep.

The following morning, when Alice and Peter left for school, Berry found itself alone in the house. It read through Alice's recipe book and decided to try one of the recipes. After finishing the recipe, Berry started reading through Peter's notes on the upcoming project for building a time machine.

Berry corrected all the mistakes in Peter's notes to ensure that the time machine would work perfectly.

When the siblings returned home, they were tired and hungry, but were overjoyed to find that Berry had prepared food for them. In gratitude, Alice made a small bed for Berry. They all ate together, and Alice and Berry went to sleep, while Peter continued to work on the time machine with the corrected notes.

After many long hours of hard work, Peter finally completed the time machine. He was thrilled and excited to invite his friends the next day to test it out, but unfortunately, they were all busy and declined the invitation. Peter felt disappointed and discouraged, but he decided to go on the journey by himself and asked Berry to join him. He instructed Alice to set the time on the machine to when he was born, and after a five-second countdown, the machine activated with a loud boom and whirring noise, which frightened Alice. However, in the midst of their journey back to twelve years ago, something went wrong. Peter realized that he had forgotten to tighten a screw that had come loose. He grew increasingly frightened as he considered the potential consequences of this mistake, and he closed his eyes tightly in fear. Suddenly, a bright flash of light filled the room, and both Peter and Berry found themselves in an entirely different place.

Suddenly, Berry began to speak to Peter, who was taken aback. "Wow! You can talk? Why didn't you ever speak to us before?" he asked in surprise.

Berry replied, "I can only speak here. This is the place where I was born, a planet called 'Olae', which means 'we will live long.'"

"I haven't heard of that name before in my science book," Peter said.

"That's because it's located right opposite the Milky Way galaxy," Berry replied. "Our galaxy is called Orion, which means 'golden life.'"

"This galaxy was created in the same way as the Milky Way galaxy," Berry continued. "Just like how you call us aliens, we call your 'region' which means 'alien' in our language. I know what mistake you made, and I have the tools in my home to fix it. Let's go there."

"Okay, let's go," Peter replied. "But I have a question. If you can breathe and live on your planet, why did you come to Earth? Did you come here to observe us so you can attack us later?"

"No, no," Berry refuted. "I actually came here with my brother, but I lost him. When I was searching for him, you found me, took me home, and took good care of me. I appreciate that. Thanks!"

"Welcome, but please help me fix my machine," Peter replied. "It's getting late, and Alice is alone."

Berry agreed, and they went to Berry's home where Berry was overjoyed to find her brother there. She narrated what had happened after she was left alone and introduced Peter, saying what a good person he was.

They went to Berry's room, and Peter was surprised to find many books that Berry had read. They collected the things they needed to fix the machine and set to work repairing it.

While fixing the machine, Berry said, "We used to think that people on Earth were so cruel that inlyu doesn't exist on Earth."

Peter asked, "What's inlyu?"

Berry replied, "That's what you call humanity."

Peter said, "Oh, yes. Not all people are bad. Many are really good at heart."

Now that they had fixed the machine, Peter was all set to go back to Earth. He started up the machine again. Berry waved Goodbye to Peter and disappeared into thin air.

After arriving back on Earth, Peter felt a sense of relief and accomplishment, felt a little sad that he had to say goodbye to Berry. Alice was also saddened by Berry's departure and shed a few tears. She asked Peter why Berry had to leave, and Peter took the time to explain the whole story to her. He emphasized the importance of being kind and humble, just like their little extraterrestrial friend. Eventually, they all went to bed, reflecting on the amazing adventure they had just experienced.

The next day, they headed to school, where Alice aced her maths exam and Peter impressed the judges with his machine, winning both prizes and money. Later that day, when they returned home, their parents had arrived and upon hearing the good news, they were filled with joy and pride for their children's accomplishments. To celebrate, they all went out to a restaurant for dinner. However, throughout the evening, Peter and Alice miss Berry, who was not with them.

To honor their beloved memory, Alice made a stuffed toy out of clothes that looked just like Berry, while Peter planted a beautiful plant in the backyard, dedicating it to Berry's memory.

They also decided to celebrate the day they found Berry as Berry's birthday and started an annual tradition of giving back to their community by donating food, clothing, and toys to those in need, remembering their humanity and the love that Berry brought to their lives.

***

“Exploration knows no bounds, and the thirst for discovery is part of what makes us human.”

– Buzz Aldrin

ADONIA POSTULATE

WRITTEN BY

MAHAUVALAKSHMI T.G.

CLASS - 9

LITTLE FLOWER PUBLIC SCHOOL
TIRUNELVELI TAMILNADU

3

ADONIA POSTULATE

"The postulate of the existence of the natural world, as a thing of independent existence and ultimate reality, is the first and greatest act of faith of the scientist."

– E.T. Bell

Year 8099 was a time when World War III ravaged the earth, causing widespread bloodshed and the use of nuclear weapons that even affected the space system. Eventually, the war ended in the year 9001. However, the aftermath of the war left only a handful of living beings in the world. The planet was divided into two major countries, NICHOLAS (Northern Hemisphere) and CLAUDE (Southern Hemisphere). The war taught people the importance of unity, and as a result, caste, religion, and other such systems were eliminated. Every citizen in the world believed in the sacredness of their motherland.

As time progressed towards the year 10204, Nicholas, led by Bree, excelled in physiology but lagged behind in astronomy. On the other hand, Claude, led by Audrey, excelled in astronomy but struggled in physiology. Despite these differences, citizens of the world were happy and content. The whole world was governed by an advanced artificial intelligence system. Both Bree and Audrey led their respective countries in the right direction, and the people were satisfied with their governance, laws, and methods of controlling the country.

Once a year, Claude country would send an astronaut to inspect and maintain the conditions of outer space. On the 5th of January 10205, the renowned astronauts Adonia, Axel, and Billy were sent to space aboard the SLA-24 rocket with the consent of Bree and Audrey. The rocket launched successfully into space, and the astronomy team closely monitored its condition while communicating with the astronauts.

While carrying out their tasks, the three astronauts began exploring various celestial bodies such as satellites, the surface of the Earth, and asteroids. However, Adonia's curiosity led her to venture out of the rocket with an oxygen cylinder to observe the surface of the sun and study cosmic rays. This made Axel and Billy uneasy, as they were concerned that the intense heat would harm Adonia's bones and internal organs.

Despite the warnings from the chief of the astronomy team, Adonia chose to ignore the advice and ventured closer to the surface of the red giant ball. She inserted her ear plugs and continued her research. This action made the astronomy team very anxious and concerned for her safety.

Adonia moved even closer to the sun's surface, coming within twenty feet of it. She could feel the warmth and her skin began to take on a light reddish hue. To her amazement, she found that the cosmic rays did not harm her. After spending six months in space, Adonia returned to Earth along with her colleagues Axel and Billy. They submitted their reports on their findings to the relevant authorities.

In his report, Axel noted that there were approximately six thousand satellites orbiting around the Earth in the satellite orbit.

In his report, Billy stated that the lander was conducting research to determine whether there were any existing water bodies on Jupiter.

In her report, Adonia mentioned that there was a fault in the space system.

Upon returning to Earth, Adonia was taken to Nicholas for medical treatment. The doctors tested her skin and overall body, but found that the cosmic rays had not caused any harmful effects, and she had not suffered from radiation sickness. This amazed the doctors, and Adonia's medical report and her hypothesis provided further evidence that there was indeed a fault in the space system.

The astronomers began conducting research into the fault in the space system, with a particular focus on cosmic rays. However, despite their efforts, they were unable to identify the root cause of the problem. A few years later, the Earth began experiencing exponential changes, and many citizens were diagnosed with vitamin D deficiency diseases. It was discovered that the Earth was no longer receiving adequate amounts of radiant and thermal energy, which was having adverse effects on the health of its inhabitants.

After extensive research, the astronomy team finally discovered the root cause of the fault in the space system. They found that in the Nebula, two helium atoms had failed to fuse, which prevented the formation of new stars. As a result, the sun was expected to disappear in the near future. When the astronomy team announced their findings in a press conference, the news caused widespread panic and despair. However, their words also inspired a sense of optimism among people, who believed that the team would be able to find a solution to the problem before it was too late.

Despite the difficulties they faced, the astronomy team was determined to find a solution to the problem. They believed that it might be possible to create an artificial sun since it was difficult to fuse hydrogen atoms in the Nebula. To fund their project, they invested millions of Satue (the currency of Nicholas and Claude). The team conducted numerous experiments, but unfortunately, their efforts were unsuccessful.

Now it's the year of '10210'. As the deadline approached and only five years remained until the sun was set to vanish, a breakthrough was finally achieved. Scientist John submitted a record of his experiment, which was approved by the astronomy team. With renewed hope, they began working on John's project in earnest.

In the year 10213, scientists were able to create an artificial sun by using a magnetic field to fuse hot plasma, which allegedly reached temperatures over one hundred and fifty million degrees Celsius. After years of work, they were finally able to launch the artificial sun at the center of our solar system via the ASP-1 rocket on January 11th, 10244.

Upon inspecting the real sun, it appeared too small and not as hot as it once was. The presence of the artificial sun, however, had stabilized the solar system and allowed for the continuation of life on Earth.

The day that the artificial sun was launched, January 11th, 10244, was a momentous occasion for humanity. It was celebrated as a new year and dubbed "World Happiness Day" by the people. Adonia, the visionary leader who spearheaded the project, was honored with the highest award of the country.

The astronomy team, led by Scientist John, was also given great esteem for their hard work and dedication in making the project a success. The award ceremony took place in the grand stadium of Neoga, situated on the golden soil of Claude. Dignitaries from all over the world attended the auspicious occasion, witnessing a moment in history that would forever be remembered.

With the launch of the artificial sun, the world became a more peaceful, blissful, and beautiful place, as the threat of certain doom had been averted. The future was brighter than ever before, and humanity could look forward to new possibilities and achievements in the years to come.

***

The Sun
Vanished
Written By
Adnan
Nadeem Khan
REG. NO. - VSFSWC-20220001
Class - 7
Indian School Al-Ghubra
Muscat, Oman
© Team Velocity

4

THE SUN VANISHED

"The solar system is a complex and fascinating place, and the more we learn about it, the more we are in awe of its beauty and complexity."

– John M. Grunsfeld

A massive spaceship, larger than the size of our Sun, has entered our solar system without any communication or warning to Earth. The spacecraft is believed to be from a distant galaxy, where extraterrestrial beings reside. The purpose of the ship's arrival is to take the Sun, which is the center of our solar system. The aliens have a powerful machine named Tyson that is capable of containing the Sun to transport it to their galaxy. The Sun is the only celestial body that keeps all the planets in our solar system in orbit around it.

After the Sun was taken from its position, all the planets in the solar system, including Mars, Jupiter, Saturn, Venus, and others, were thrown out of their orbits and began to drift aimlessly through the universe. Without any gravitational control, Earth too is now adrift in the vast expanse of space. As a result, there are parts of Earth where it is still daytime and the Sun can be seen perfectly, while in other areas, darkness prevails. However, nobody on Earth is aware of the theft of the Sun, which is a crucial element in our solar system, and the chaos that has resulted from it.

Although the aliens have already taken the Sun from our solar system, we are still able to see its light on Earth for around 8 minutes and 20 seconds. This is because it takes that amount of time for the Sun's light to travel the vast distance between the Sun and Earth. Therefore, even though the Sun has been taken, we are still able to observe its light as it reaches us from the past position of the Sun.

After 8 minutes and 20 seconds

The Earth suddenly plunged into darkness, and night fell instantaneously. The stars could be seen clearly as there was no longer any light from the Sun to obscure them. The Moon and other planets also disappeared from view. The effects of this event will be most pronounced on plants and trees, which rely on the Sun's light for the process of photosynthesis. Without the Sun's light, plants are unable to produce oxygen, which is essential for their survival as well as that of other organisms that rely on them. This sudden loss of sunlight will have a significant impact on the entire ecosystem, causing widespread disruption and potentially leading to long-term consequences for life on Earth.

1 Hour Later

As more than an hour has passed, more than half of the world's population remains confused and shocked by the sudden darkness that has descended on the planet. People in places where it is normally daytime have also now realized that it is night, adding to the confusion. As a consequence of the loss of sunlight, the temperature is slowly dropping, but the Earth's core is helping to regulate it, keeping it from becoming too extreme. However, the sudden change in temperature and the lack of sunlight will have far-reaching impacts on the climate, weather patterns, and ecosystems across the globe, leading to unpredictable consequences for the future of life on Earth.

24 Hours Later

After 24 hours, people are still hoping for help and looking for answers to the sudden disappearance of the Sun. It is morning, but there is no sign of the Sun rising. The government and authorities are unable to do anything to resolve the situation as it is beyond human control. The temperature has dropped drastically, with some places experiencing a temperature of 8°C, causing plants and animals to become weak and vulnerable. However, in some areas, there is still residual heat due to the Earth's atmosphere absorbing some heat from the Sun, which may last for another three to four days. The future looks uncertain, and people are left wondering what will happen next and how they will survive in a world without the Sun.

7 days later

Seven days have passed since the Sun disappeared, and the world is still shrouded in darkness. The temperature has dropped even further, reaching a bone-chilling -15°C. As a result, water has frozen, and most of it is now in solid form. With the loss of the Sun, the satellites that provide TV and internet service are no longer functioning, leading to a complete blackout of information and communication. Additionally, the dams that generate electricity have frozen over, causing a widespread power outage. This has made it impossible for people to call their loved ones and has created a sense of isolation and despair.

The lack of sunlight has taken its toll on the ecosystem, and most of the trees and plants have died. In response to the extreme conditions, the government has started building basements where people can seek shelter and stay warm. With no sense of time and no clear solution in sight, people are struggling to survive in this new, harsh reality.

1 Month Later

After one month, the situation on Earth has worsened significantly. The temperature has plummeted to an unbearable -40°C, causing the planet to appear white from space due to the thick layer of snow and ice. All the plants, except those that can adapt to extremely cold temperatures, have died, and most animals have perished due to lack of food and the harsh conditions.

The sea is frozen, and most sea creatures have died due to the lack of access to air and food. The death of all plants has led to a significant increase in CO_2 levels in the atmosphere, making it difficult to breathe. There are only a few places where life can still be found, such as near active volcanoes, where the heat and volcanic gases provide a little warmth and nourishment. The situation is bleak, and people are struggling to survive in this new, frozen world.

1 Year Later

After one year, the situation on Earth has worsened to an unimaginable extent. All forms of life, including animals and plants, have perished due to the extreme cold and lack of food. The cities are now buried under thick layers of snow, and snow-capped mountains have formed where once there were buildings and streets.

Only one place on Earth still harbors life, and that is the Mariana Trench, the deepest part of the ocean. Some hardy species have managed to survive in the extreme depths of the trench, where the water is heated by underwater volcanoes and geothermal vents provide nutrients. However, it is unknown how long these species can survive in this inhospitable environment.

The rest of the planet is a frozen wasteland, devoid of all forms of life. The Earth's atmosphere has become so cold and thin that it is impossible for humans to survive without protective suits and equipment. The world, once a vibrant and diverse place, is now a lifeless, frozen desert.

1000 Years Later

After 1000 years, the Earth is completely unrecognizable from what it once was. The frozen planet has been transformed into a barren, lifeless wasteland. The air is thin and devoid of oxygen, making it impossible for any form of life to exist.

The snow and ice that once covered the planet have long since evaporated or been blown away, leaving behind vast stretches of rocky terrain. The few remaining structures and artifacts from human civilization have been weathered away by the harsh elements over the centuries.

The only evidence of life that remains is in the form of fossils and other remnants of the creatures that once roamed the planet. However, these are now buried deep beneath the Earth's surface, and it is unlikely that they will ever be discovered by any future civilization that may arise.

The sun, which was once the source of all life on Earth, has long since faded into the distance. It is now nothing more than a distant memory, a relic of a bygone era when the planet was teeming with life and energy. The Earth will continue to spin through the cold, dark expanse of space, a silent testament to the fleeting nature of existence.

1100 Years Later

1,100 years later, over a century has passed, and the temperature has dropped to -160°C. Earth is now situated amidst a swarm of meteors and asteroids. Suddenly, a meteor hurtles towards the planet at great speed, just five minutes away.

5 minutes Later

After five minutes, the meteor collides with Earth, obliterating all signs of life on the planet.

This story teaches us a valuable lesson: the Sun is crucial for sustaining life on Earth. Without it, our planet would be lifeless and barren. It is a precious gift from God.

ILLUSION OF TIME

WRITTEN BY

KABEER KHAN

Reg. No.- VSFSWC-20220011

CLASS- 7

BAL BHAWAN SCHOOL

BHOPAL, MADHYA PRADESH

5

ILLUSION OF TIME

"I believe that space travel will one day become as common as airline travel is today."

– Neil Armstrong

In year 2050, NASA, SpaceX, ISRO, and other space agencies embarked on a groundbreaking project: a space trip that would be open to everyone. To make this possible, they began creating millions, even billions, of spaceships. Through extensive research and preparation, the teams ensured that anyone who passed the rigorous examination would be deemed fit to embark on this incredible journey, regardless of their age, including children and the elderly. The examination process was carefully crafted to evaluate all aspects of the candidate's physical and mental preparedness, ensuring that they were equipped to handle the demands of space travel. This project represented a tremendous technological achievement, offering a unique opportunity for people of all ages to explore the mysteries of the cosmos and forge new bonds across the boundaries that divide us.

Just like everyone else, Harry dreamed of going to space and was thrilled when his dad, Steve, announced they would embark on the adventure together. At the time, Harry was only 13 years old. This ambitious project took many years to complete, and eventually, the day arrived for them to undergo the rigorous examination process. To qualify for the space trip, both Harry and Steve had to pass the exam and complete the UFO training program.

Harry dedicated five years to the demanding UFO training, and when the day finally arrived for them to embark on their space adventure, he was overflowing with excitement. Before departing, all the participants, including children, had to pass the examination and the training program, ensuring that they were well-prepared for the unique challenges of space travel. All the children had to travel with their parents or a designated guardian, ensuring their safety and well-being throughout the journey.

ꕥ

Harry and his father were assigned to the Cerus-13 spaceship, which would depart on March 2, 2055, for their highly anticipated journey to the planet Mercury. The excitement of the upcoming adventure was palpable, but so was the awareness of the risks involved in space travel.

To ensure their safety, each person traveling in space was assigned two experienced astronauts to accompany them. These professionals would provide guidance and support during the launch of the spacecraft and throughout the entire journey. This was a critical component of the overall plan, ensuring that all space travelers had the necessary resources and expertise at their disposal in case of an emergency.

As Harry and his father eagerly awaited their departure, they marveled at the enormity of the undertaking they were about to embark on. They were filled with a sense of awe and wonder at the prospect of exploring the vast expanse of space and discovering the mysteries of Mercury. At the same time, they were humbled by the enormity of the task and the knowledge that the success of their journey rested on the shoulders of many dedicated scientists, engineers, and astronauts.

As Harry, his father, and the two astronauts strapped themselves into their seats, they felt the excitement and anticipation of the lift-off. The engines roared to life and suddenly they were launched into space. The force of the lift-off was intense, and they all felt the incredible power of the spacecraft as it broke through Earth's atmosphere.

As they reached the orbit of the Earth, they gazed out the window in amazement at the stunning views of our planet from above. The experience was breathtaking, and they were all filled with a sense of wonder and awe.

However, their time in space was limited due to the fact that the food supplies on board were only sufficient for a short period. Despite the briefness of their journey, the experience was unforgettable. For Harry, his father, and everyone else on board, it was an incredible first-time experience that they could never have imagined.

Suddenly without any warning, the Cerus-13 spacecraft began to emit a strange noise and veer off course, as if pulled by some powerful, magnetic force. Harry and his father, Steve, were gripped with fear as the astronauts lost control of the ship. Suddenly, a black, circular object appeared, enveloping the spacecraft and blocking out all visibility.

"What's going on, astronauts? You assured us that this trip was safe. If it's supposed to be safe, then why is this happening? Please explain," Steve said, his voice rising with anger and frustration.

"We're not entirely sure what's happening, but based on our training, the spacecraft may be experiencing some automated functions for a short period. This is all part of the space trip experience, so let's try to enjoy it and not be too frightened," replied Astronaut Robert in a reassuring tone.

The two astronauts knew that they were in a precarious situation and that they were in danger, but they didn't inform Steve of their concerns, fearing that he would blame their company once they returned. As they continued on their journey, they spotted several planets that were vastly different from those in the Milky Way galaxy. Despite their amazement, they assumed that these planets belonged to their galaxy.

Steve asked, "How did we reach so fast?"

"The spacecraft is like this only in space. You won't feel the passage of time," said astronaut Robert.

Harry thought there might be a problem because Mercury didn't look like this in satellite photos.

The astronauts said, "Please take your seats because we're about to land on this planet."

Finally, they had successfully landed. Since Harry, his father Steve, and the astronauts already knew that there was no water or oxygen on the planet Mercury, they had brought sufficient food and water for their space trip that would last for a few months. You might think that the food would perish, but it was not stored in the same way you would keep it at home. Instead, it was in the form of energy tablets that would not expire for three years.

However, surprisingly, they were not feeling hungry. They didn't know why because they had only eaten the food when they were on Earth, so they couldn't explain why they weren't feeling any hunger.

When they stepped out of their spacecraft wearing their suits to explore the planet, they saw a vast ocean. They were surprised because they had known beforehand that there was no water on the planet.

Suddenly, one of the astronauts, Robert, said, "Come here quickly. The oxygen indicator device is showing that there is oxygen here."

They were even more confused.

Harry said, "I don't think this is our planet."

But no one believed him. They thought that there might have been some problem with the earlier research. They discussed and decided to explore the entire planet, as they had sufficient time and food. They thought that if they conducted more research, there was a chance that they would be able to confirm whether or not this was the planet Mercury.

ᔓᔕ

Now they decided to take off their space suits with much confidence because one mistake could result in the death of all. It was fine. The air was much cleaner than on Earth, which was amazing. They were shocked! They planned to travel across the entire planet to explore. They visited many areas but found no trees or any extraterrestrial organisms, which made them even more surprised.

While exploring the planet, they came across a clear black sea that frightened them. They started thinking about what Harry had said, that this was not the planet Mercury. The astronauts, along with Harry and Steve, knew that this was not Mercury because they had already conducted research on that planet and there was no such black sea. They had explored the entire Mercury planet.

Steve said, "This is not the planet Mercury. How can there be oxygen without trees, and how can water exist here? We should go back to Earth and inform them about it."

Robert said, "Yes, you are right, Mr. Steve. We should lift off now from here. There is not enough time, and we don't know what is present on this planet. There could be many extraterrestrial animals in this planet that may be dangerous for us. We should leave immediately. Let's go."

They reached the spacecraft and started it immediately. But suddenly, a beeping sound was heard, indicating that the fuel tank was empty.

"Empty fuel! What? How did this happen? Please start the lift-off," Steve said.

"I don't know what's happening. I think the fuel tank is empty, but how it happened, I don't know," Robert said.

"We have not used the fuel that much, so how could it be empty?" Steve questioned.

"I think we should go to the fuel tank and see what has happened; otherwise, we'll just keep thinking and won't be able to find a solution. It is a new planet, and there could be anything," Robert said.

"Yes, you are right," Steve agreed.

☙

They were all very upset, especially Harry. Steve and Robert went to check the fuel tank. When they saw the fuel tank, they found it full of some unknown extraterrestrial organisms that looked like eels.

Robert and Steve understood that these extraterrestrial organisms had consumed all the fuel. These organisms were different from any known type of organism, as they were capable of drinking fuel. Now, as they had nothing left, they were stranded and helpless without fuel. They couldn't go anywhere. After some time, their food would also be finished, and only water would be left.

Harry said to his father Steve, "Dad, if there is oxygen and water, there must be life too. I think there are more animals like those unknown creatures we saw."

Steve replied, "Yes, that's possible, but we haven't seen any others yet except for those eel-like creatures."

Harry then asked, "So dad, what are we going to do now?"

Steve sighed and replied, "I don't know what the solution to this problem is."

Robert was an experienced person at NASA and had been working there for more than a decade, so he knew more about science than anyone else on the team. He thought for a moment and then said, "I think there might be fuel on this planet."

Steve asked, "How do you know that?"

Robert replied, "Well, as those eel-like creatures were drinking fuel so quickly, and they seem to have the ability to locate fuel simply by smell, it's possible that they have consumed this type of fuel before."

Steve said, "You are somewhat right. Whether there is fuel or not, it doesn't matter. We should go and find fuel."

"Okay. So I think we should leave tomorrow," Robert said.

Harry said, "No, not tomorrow, because a day here is only 5 hours long."

Robert said, "Ohh! I really forgot about that."

They began their journey towards the fuel source without knowing for certain whether it was present or not. Undeterred, they pressed on, leaving their spaceship behind and taking all their supplies, including food. Along the way, they discovered caves where they decided to rest for the night. However, they were surprised to see conical structures made of solid material that were gradually melting.

Robert asked, "What is this liquid substance that is coming from it?"

Steve reassured, "These are just some types of rocks found on this planet. There's nothing to be afraid of, let's just get some sleep."

They all went to sleep, but Robert was awakened by a drip-drop sound. He couldn't shake off the thought and decided to investigate. As he approached the conical substance, he detected the unmistakable smell of fuel. Upon touching and smelling it, he was certain that it was indeed fuel. Realizing the significance of their discovery, he quickly woke up the rest of the group and shared the news. Excitement filled the air as they eagerly anticipated their return to Earth after being stranded for so many days.

"Listen, if there is fuel here, there might also be creatures that could pose a threat to us. It's best if we leave this place immediately," Steve said.

Suddenly, an animal attacked them, causing them to flee from the cave.

"I believe that the animal only attacks when it hears a sound. It also seems to have poor eyesight since it didn't attack us when we stood still," Steve said.

"I was thinking the same thing. We should try to retrieve the fuel silently. Steve and I can go, while Harry and John stay here. Is that okay, Steve?" Robert suggested.

"Yes, that sounds like a plan," Steve agreed.

They quickly retrieved the fuel and rushed back towards their spacecraft.

"We need to take off as quickly as possible once we reach the spacecraft. If we wait around, those animals might attack us again and we'll be in trouble," Robert advised.

"Absolutely, we should make haste," Steve agreed.

Upon reaching the spacecraft, they promptly refueled the tank and even stocked up on extra fuel for emergencies. With the tank filled to the brim, they initiated lift-off and soon the spacecraft was soaring through space.

ᔓ

As they journeyed through the vast expanse of the universe, they were unsure of their destination. However, a sudden flash of bright white light interrupted their thoughts. The intense brightness made it difficult for them to keep their eyes open. Once the light faded, they found themselves gazing upon the beautiful blue planet they had left behind - Earth.

"It looked just like Earth, maybe it is Earth," Steve mused.

"I have a feeling that it is indeed Earth and we are headed back to our home planet. It's a miracle," Robert exclaimed in disbelief.

They landed on the planet without having a clear idea of their location, driven by a strong desire to reunite with their families. Strangely, there was no signal or communication from the outside world. They were uncertain of where to land, but eventually, they managed to land on water.

Upon stepping outside, they were met with a scene of intense depression and very few people around. They were surprised to see various robots and machines scattered around. Confused and desperate to find answers, they approached a person and asked where the head of NASA was located.

To their surprise, the person responded with anger and accused them of asking silly questions. The person even suggested they should have used telepathy to communicate.

Robert was taken aback by the person's response and explained that they had just come from Mercury and were in trouble. However, the person remained uncooperative and directed them to ask the robot for answers instead.

The person said something in their mind, and the robot police came and arrested them all. They were arrested by NASA because the word "NASA" was written on the guards' t-shirts. The police officer was human, but everyone else was a robot.

The officer asked the astronauts and Steve, "Who are you people, and why are you doing these nonsensical things? Are you mad?"

Robert said, "Sir, we are astronauts, and he is Steve & his son, Harry. Sir, we only want to tell you that we are not dangerous people. We have just come back from a space trip, but we were lost in space during that trip. Now, we have ended up here."

The police officer said, "What? A space trip? That's impossible! Space trips have been banned for a year. Do you think I am mad?"

Robert said, "Sir, you can check our spaceship. It's a Cerus-13 model from the year 2050."

The police officer said, "Cerus-13? Now, you're making me even more confused. I'll call a scientist, and he will talk to you."

The scientist arrived and saw Steve and Harry. He was surprised and said, "Are you Steve? Are you Harry?"

Steve said, "Yes, we are. How do you know us?"

The scientist hugged them and cried and cried.

The scientist said to the police officer, "These people are not criminals. They are the people from the Cerus-13 spacecraft who were lost."

The police officer asked, "Sir, how did they end up here? It's not possible to survive in space for 30 years, is it?"

"I don't know either. I will ask them," replied the scientist.

☙

The scientist said to Steve, "Steve, I am Henry, the scientist. I am your friend Henry. We don't know how you survived or what you did to survive. This is the year 2080, and you are here. Tell us how you came here and why your age has not been affected."

Steve looked at the man standing in front of him, confused. "Are you that Henry?" he asked. "How is that possible? You were not so old. How could this happen? Are you serious?"

"Yes, I am Henry. I also don't know what happened to you in 2050 when your spacecraft disappeared. We searched the entire galaxy, but you were nowhere to be found," replied Henry.

"I don't know anything either. When we were on Earth, it was 2050, and when we went on the space trip, I didn't want to go, but you convinced me. Suddenly, a white light appeared, and we were lost. I thought we had reached the planet Mercury, but it was something else. There was oxygen but no trees, and the days were only five hours long. We survived only because of oxygen. When we tried to lift off, there was no fuel due to some extraterrestrial organism that looked like ills. We found fuel on another planet and quickly launched from there. In space, we saw a white light again and then couldn't see anything. When the light vanished, we saw planet Earth, and we came here. Then this police officer arrested us," explained Steve.

"I don't understand how you came to the year 2080. There are two ways of time travel: traveling into a black hole or traveling at the speed of light. We have tried both methods with high-tech technology, but we were still unable to achieve time travel. So, how did you do it? In 2050, we didn't have such advanced technology. I think that the white light was a black hole, but why weren't you spaghettified?" questioned Henry.

"I don't know anything. Please help us, Henry. I have to go back to my time," pleaded Steve.

"Listen, this world is coming to an end, and we are about to die because of the black hole. We have done everything that was possible. Some humans have moved to other galaxies, and some went to other planets with oxygen. But some humans, like me, have stayed behind to manage everything and to manage the robots," said Henry.

Steve asked, "Why haven't you gone? You will die here."

"If I were to die, what would happen? Go back to your time and inform everyone so that nothing happens. Listen, there is very little time left. You may only be able to save the world with this harmful ultra-supermassive black hole. I think you arrived from a very small black hole that only appears sometimes and is very rarely seen. You have time-traveled by accident, but you have done it. Don't do it again. Go back to your time and tell everyone about this. Please leave now and take my spacecraft. It is high-tech and you can leave through the small black hole only, otherwise you will die. Please save the world, otherwise human civilization will be destroyed." said Henry.

"But I cannot leave you behind," pleaded Steve.

"You can only save me by going into the past and saving my younger self. Please, go…go," urged Henry.

Steve asked, "Why can't you come with us?"

"If I were to go with you, my other self from the past and present will merge, and it will create a paradox. It could have catastrophic consequences on the timeline. Please go alone and save the world," explained Henry.

ଓ

Robert, Steve, Harry, and John understood everything, and they launched their spacecraft. Soon they were out of the Earth's atmosphere. It was disheartening to see the Earth getting destroyed by the black hole. They passed through the small black hole without any issues.

Upon reaching their destination, they found themselves in the year 2050.

After reaching the year 2050, they told the full story of what had happened. They shared everything about their time-traveling adventure, the ultra-supermassive black hole, meeting Henry, and his plea for them to save the world. They also explained how they used Henry's spacecraft to travel back in time and prevent the black hole from causing the destruction of human civilization.

Although their story seemed unbelievable, they provided evidence to support their claims, and people began to believe them. However, as they looked around, they noticed that nothing had changed, and everything seemed the same as before. It was as if nothing had happened.

It is true that the concept of time can be complex and difficult to understand, especially when combined with the effects of a black hole. The laws of physics and space-time can seem like an illusion, but they are the foundation of our universe. The experience of Robert, Steve, Harry, and John is a reminder of the mystery and wonder of the universe, and the importance of scientific exploration and understanding.

***

THE UNIVERSE CONNECTS

WRITTEN BY

PRISHA ARORA

CLASS – 9

Delhi Public School, Bopal
Ahmedabad, Gujarat

REG. NO.- VSFSWC-202220059

6

THE UNIVERSE CONNECTS

"Life isn't about finding yourself. Life is about creating yourself."

– George Bernard Shaw

I was teasing my younger sister, Binny, who is two years younger than me and only eight years old. She had developed a bump on her head over the last few days, and I couldn't resist poking fun at her. However, my teasing quickly backfired when she retaliated by pulling my hair. I must admit that I am not always the best sister to her, but I couldn't help but enjoy teasing her and running my fingers through her hair as we lay in bed together. Sadly, this was just a typical night for us.

But who knew the next few days were not going to be as usual. Binny woke up complaining about pain in her head. Mom took her to the doctor, and after examining her, the doctor prescribed some medicines.

Days went by, but the bump on Binny's head followed by the persistent headache refused to disappear. Our parents decided to take her to the largest hospital in town, where the doctors conducted various tests and x-rays. Finally, the doctor delivered the shocking news - Binny had a tumour in her head, an abnormality that was deemed fatal. The news left me in utter shock, and for the next few days, I was in denial. Although my parents were doing their best, it seemed like it was not enough to tackle this devastating situation.

One week after the diagnosis, my parents returned from the hospital looking exhausted, and I could see defeat in their eyes. Suddenly, tears welled up in my eyes, and I ran back to my room. Binny was sleeping there, so peaceful and innocent. Seeing her like that, I couldn't hold back my tears any longer. I gazed out of the window, praying, hoping, and calling out to the universe for help. I prayed for Binny's life, her well-being, and her recovery. It pained me to think that I had made fun of her bump, and I felt guilty for not being a better sister to her.

Suddenly, a sharp, bright light appeared out of nowhere and moved towards me. It came closer and stopped, and the light faded away to reveal a young woman with gentle eyes and a kind face. I wasn't scared of her, even though I had no idea where she came from. She introduced herself and said that she knew about Binny's condition and could help her. Her words filled me with hope, and I sensed that it wasn't a dream. It felt real. She went on to explain that she had traveled from the future using a time machine and that I would understand why she came to help when the time came. She added that she would take Binny with her, perform a surgery with the help of other doctors, and bring her back by morning.

Something miraculous happened that gave me a reason to believe it was all real. I was desperate to save my sister, and this mysterious woman offered me hope. She took little Binny in her arms and disappeared into a bright light. The next morning, I woke up next to Binny, and I desperately searched my memories, trying to recall what had happened the night before. Was it all just a dream?

I felt relieved that it wasn't a dream when I saw Binny's miraculous improvement in the next few days. Only I knew the truth about what had happened, but I kept it to myself as nobody would have believed me. All I cared about was that my little Binny was back to her old self again, and I was grateful for whatever had happened to make her better.

৩

Year 2022, it's been forty years since that miraculous night when my little sister Binny was saved by a mysterious woman from the future. To this day, I still don't fully understand how it happened. Time machines remain the stuff of stories and dreams, and yet, I know what I saw was real. Lost in thought, I suddenly receive an urgent call to perform an emergency surgery at the hospital. A pregnant woman has been in a serious accident and is in critical condition. Without hesitation, I rush to perform my duty as a doctor, a calling that has been my life ever since the day Binny was saved by a doctor. It's my little way of paying back the universe for the miracle that saved my sister's life.

After a long surgery, the baby was delivered safely, but the woman remained critical. I looked into the baby's innocent eyes and felt them calling out to the universe for help. The next day, I received the relieving news of the woman's recovery. I visited her and she thanked me for saving her baby and giving her the gift of being able to see her.

"I vaguely asked her, 'What name have you thought of for the beautiful baby girl?'

Her eyes twinkled and she replied, 'She is my little Sneha.'

Sneha, there is something familiar about this name. I thought, 'Well, it's a pretty common name,' but later, something struck me. Ah! Sneha!

I remembered!

'I am Dr. Sneha and have come from the year 2055.' This was the angel's introduction to me years back, the angel who saved Binny's life."

***

"In three words I can sum up everything
I've learned about life: it goes on."

– Robert Frost

THE MISSING
GIRL
WRITTEN BY
KASHISH MOURYA
CLASS – 7
REG. NO.- VSFSWC-20220019
Maharishi Vidya Mandir
Raipur, Chhattisgarh
© Team Velocity
SCHOOL

7

THE MISSING GIRL

"Human emotions are a powerful force. They can drive us to create beauty, to fight for justice, or to love with all our hearts."

– Melinda Gates

On August 20, 2018, I attended my friend Riya's 12th birthday party. Riya and I were both in 7th grade at Maharshi Vidya Mandir School and shared a close bond. She had a fascination for science and loved to talk about aliens, always eager to explain them to me.

I arrived at the party at 7 p.m. The hotel where my friend's birthday party was being held was very big, with a large party lawn. When I arrived, I saw that everyone was enjoying the party. I went over to my friend and wished her a happy birthday, saying, "Happy Birthday, Riya!"

After some time, I noticed that my friend was missing. At first, I didn't pay much attention to it, but then I realized it was getting late and everyone was waiting for her to cut the cake. I started feeling a bit upset and began searching for her.

I went to the forest behind the hotel in search of my friend who had gone missing. In the distance, I saw a bright light and as I approached it, I discovered a large spaceship parked nearby.

When I saw the spaceship, I started thinking that my friend might be inside. I cautiously entered the spaceship and to my surprise, I saw some aliens inside. Fear crept up on me as I wondered if my friend was with them. My worry for her grew.

The aliens were speaking in their own language, which I could not understand at first. Then I looked at my watch, which had a feature to translate any language. The anxiety in my heart subsided, and I pressed the language button on my magical watch. Now my watch was translating everything for me, and I was able to understand what the aliens were saying.

I was really shocked after learning about what the aliens were planning to do. They had started making a clone of my friend Riya, who was fast asleep on a cloudy bed surrounded by some green rays. Two of the aliens were busy making Riya's clone.

I was secretly listening to their conversation and carefully observing everything. They had a five-year plan for their mission or project. Within a few seconds, the clone of my friend was standing upright. I became very curious to know what they were planning to do with this clone of my dear friend Riya.

The next moment, they sent the cloned Riya out of the spaceship and took my original friend Riya with them.

Clone Riya was now moving towards the party hall. I was spying on her to see what she was going to do next. But I was surprised because she behaved so naturally, just like my friend, the original Riya. I even spoke with her, and she seemed like Riya. But then I wondered who was the person they had taken with them?

"After a while, I noticed that this was not my friend Riya, but the clone Riya, as she did not have the tattoo on her left wrist, which my friend had. I thought about sharing this whole situation with my parents or Riya's parents, but I couldn't find a way to prove myself. Despite trying a lot, I failed to share this with anyone."

I now realized that the aliens didn't want to harm anyone in their plan. They intended to leave the clone of my friend Riya on Earth and take the original Riya with them, possibly to gather information about our planet Earth.

Now, as the clone Riya cut the cake, everyone was clapping and singing "Happy Birthday to you Riya... Happy Birthday to you". She received many gifts, but there was no sign of happiness on her face. I closely observed her, knowing that she was not my original friend Riya.

—

Now, from the next day onwards, the clone Riya started living and doing everything like the original Riya. We attended school together and enjoyed our time. Years passed by like this, and the clone Riya lived a good life. I never thought of sharing anything about her with anyone because she was a good person.

As time passed, I noticed that the clone Riya was slowly starting to develop her own personality and interests. She was not just a copy of my friend

Riya anymore, but a unique individual with her own thoughts and feelings. It was fascinating to watch her grow and discover new things about herself and the world around her. Even though she was not the original Riya, I couldn't help but feel grateful for her presence in my life. She had become a dear friend to me in her own right.

Over time, the clone Riya had become an integral part of the family. She had her own personality, her own likes and dislikes, and had developed close relationships with everyone in the family. She had become especially close to Riya's younger brother, who had always looked up to his older sister.

Clone Riya was an excellent student, just like the original Riya, and she excelled in all her subjects. She was also an accomplished athlete and participated in various sports competitions. She had even won several awards and accolades for her achievements.

At home, Clone Riya was a great help to Riya's parents, and often took charge of household responsibilities. She was a good cook and enjoyed experimenting with new recipes. She was also a skilled musician and often played the guitar in her free time. Her love for music was infectious, and she had even taught Riya's parents how to play some basic chords.

Despite her many accomplishments, Clone Riya often felt a sense of unease, as if she was living a lie. She knew that she was not the real Riya, and sometimes felt guilty for taking her place. But she had grown to love her life on Earth and had come to accept her role as the clone.

After 5 years

As the years passed, the clone Riya continued to live a life as close to the original Riya as possible. She had now reached in class-12 and was studying hard for her exams. She had her own set of friends and had even developed a unique personality that was slightly different from the original Riya. However, she still had a sense of detachment and always felt like something was missing in her life. Even though she had the same experiences and memories as Riya, she knew deep down that she was not the real Riya.

As the board exams of class-12 approached, the clone Riya became more anxious and worried about her performance. She knew that her grades would determine her future and she wanted to make the original Riya proud.

We were getting ready for our class 12 board exams, which were scheduled to start at 9 a.m. Suddenly, I noticed that the clone Riya was missing again. Worried about her, I started searching and eventually found myself at the back of our school. And there it was, after so many years, the same spaceship that had brought the aliens who created the clone of my friend Riya.

As I approached the spaceship, I overheard the aliens discussing their plans to take the clone Riya with them and return the original Riya. The leader of the group announced, "Our research on humans and their way of life on Earth is now complete. It is time to return this beautiful girl, Riya, to her rightful place with her parents."

But the problem now was that the clone Riya was not willing to go back with the aliens. She spoke to them and said, "I love the life I have here on Earth with my friends and family. I do not want to go back to our planet. I am happy here with my friends."

The aliens tried to explain to the clone Riya that, "You are not the real Riya, but a clone created by us for research purposes. We left you here to take the place of Riya so that we could complete our mission. Our research is now complete, and it is time for you to come back with us. However, you may be allowed to stay on Earth only if Riya agrees to manage with you."

The clone Riya discussed with the original Riya, explaining her desire to stay on Earth with her family and friends. The original Riya understood the clone's feelings and hugged her, promising to find a way to help her stay. After much thought, the original Riya came up with a plan: the clone Riya would need to become invisible in order to stay on Earth without drawing unwanted attention. She explained that only she would be able to see the clone, but the clone would be able to see everyone else. The clone Riya agreed to the plan, grateful for the chance to continue her life on Earth.

Finally, as the spaceship took off, both the clone Riya and the original Riya ran towards their home. They are now living happily on earth, with the clone Riya remaining invisible to everyone except for the original Riya. It was a happy ending to a strange and surreal experience that changed their lives forever.

***

"Every living organism is constantly
evolving, constantly changing,
constantly adapting. That's what it
means to be alive, to pass on your genes
to the next generation."

– Neil deGrasse Tyson

Grandma's Genetic Wit

WRITTEN BY

N. HANIYA ZAHRAA
REG. NO.- VSFSWC-20220059
CLASS - 9
LITTLE FLOWER PUBLIC SCHOOL
TIRUNELVELI , TAMIL NADU

8

GRANDMA'S GENETIC WIT

"Grandmother. The true power behind the power."

– Lisa Birnbach

It was a brand new day with charming sunlight streaming through the window of our protagonist's house. Eira woke up feeling sleepy but with a whole lot of expectations. Before I continue writing about her, I would like to share her flashback with you.

A tall, pretty woman stepped out of the Swiss Federal Institute of Technology in Zurich, holding her graduate paper and wearing a big black coat that was larger than her size. Her name was Caria, and she had completed her degree in biology in 1820. Although her native place was Nagercoil, she was sent there for a better education. Caria was born into a family of landlords and was considered their little princess. She loved her family more than anything in the world. However, because her family valued her safety the most, they decided to get her married to a man named Huzaifa at a very young age. Nevertheless, she had full support from her family.

After this special occasion, Caria moved to Zurich and began working in a biological research center. Her parents were happy for her. Her research indicated that each modified form of DNA conveys different information about a creature. Since people would never believe anything blindly, she worked on gathering proof. In addition, at the age of 25, Caria had two daughters, Emelia and Nitona. Unfortunately, before she could complete her research, Caria passed away at the age of 62, leaving behind a granddaughter named Eira. Prior to her death, Caria transformed her own DNA into Eira, hoping that she would either complete the research or find some type of proof. Furthermore, she wrote a brief summary of her ideas and thoughts and packed them away in the attic of her house. These two actions proved to be a blessing for Eira.

She soon grew up to be a young girl with long hair, adorable dresses, and a face and character that resembled Caria's. She was home-schooled by her parents and did not have much knowledge about society and the environment, but she was a great listener and quick learner. Her dreams were different, and so was she. Eira had now completed the same research as Caria, but she had started researching tombs and mummies.

During the festive season, her house had to be repainted, and she was assigned to clean the attic where she found Caria's belongings. She spent the whole day reading through them, and by night, she had completed her job, taken a shower, filled her tummy, and was ready to go to sleep. She had different dreams, but managed to sleep peacefully, except for one dream that haunted her regularly. It was like a particle combining with another to form a molecule. She knew that it was conveying something to her, but in her busy schedule, she did not want to waste time on it.

Her goal was to create a legacy in which future generations would speak of her. Eira started her job with King Kitara of Fab's family, who died of a mysterious disease. She obtained permission from the Egyptian government and began collecting preservation powders and stones for her project, which was the process of becoming an Egyptologist. As a student, she was given one week to access the tomb.

However, a wretched part of her life occurred: her father passed away. He had been her greatest support, motivation, backbone, and more. It took her nearly three days to free herself from those melancholic feelings, but once the funeral function was completed, she had only two days left to complete her project. She rushed to collect the samples, but her mind was preoccupied with her father and his new illness.

She was a little relieved when she found lice on King Kitara's head, as it would be a great advantage for her project. The blood was in a frozen state, and she collected all her samples and left the tomb by half-past five in the evening. She referred to books about DNA and sought help from her warm-hearted professor.

Her biological graduation had been a great benefit for her, and she began to research blood samples from her father before he died, as well as samples from the tomb. While her research was in process, the nation was in a state of great alert due to an infectious microbe that suppressed the digestive system, preventing people from intaking food and leading to death. The disease was named Filstrent.

Every day, she went to her lab with all necessary precautionary measures. Her life was going like a straight road with no vehicles travelling in it. She usually listened to the radio while travelling and noticed that it was a virus. To derive medicine for it, she needed to know its initial state, but this virus had only affected people in recent times. Ancient people may have been affected by its initial stage, but they didn't have any idea about it.

Three days passed, and on the fourth day, she was surprised to see the results of her research that showed her father was affected by the disease that was cursing the nation and that had a great matching with the samples of blood from the tomb. She then researched more deeply and finally found that King Kitatra was affected by the initial stage of the virus. What a coincidence! As it was difficult to come up with a vaccine for the virus and to safeguard the body so the microbe would never affect the body again, she got help from her peers. She tested it with a species or creature she had to ensure it wouldn't cause any side effects, and it was successful.

She brought it to public attention and it was approved by the World Health Organization (WHO). People began to receive the vaccine and were now free from the disease, enjoying good health. The population experienced a great relief from the curse of the disease, and the media began to praise her after she spoke to the press, mentioning her peers, Caria, and her diary, as well as the DNA she had transferred.

Congratulations to her and her peer for receiving the Laskar award for their contributions to medicine!

It's wonderful to see their hard work and dedication being recognized and celebrated by the nation. This also serves as proof to Caria's statement and highlights the importance of scientific research and collaboration in finding solutions to health problems.

REG. NO.- VSFSWC-20220123
© Team Velocity
THE SPACE WAR
WRITTEN BY
Khushboo Kannaujiya
CLASS - 12
GURU NANAK ENGLISH MEDIUM SCHOOL
VARANASI, UTTAR PRADESH

9

THE SPACE WAR

"You can pray and fight at the same time, Corporal. Especially if you learn how before things get rough. It's important to have a philosophy of life ... and of death."

– Henry V. O'Neil

We are not alone in this universe; there are other creatures who may look like us or be totally different from us. After many years of hard work, our scientists have found a planet on which life is possible, named 'Valkyria'. In the pictures sent by the satellite, some objects were seen moving, and their temperature was also increasing or decreasing with time. This moment is full of wonder, a great achievement for the entire human race. To further strengthen this proof, a seven-member team has been formed by the 'Space Boost' organization. This organization is a group of capable scientists from all over the world who enable mankind to fight against every challenge. The mission on Valkyria is to explore the environment there and collect information about the species present.

For the first time in human history, the command of a mission is not in the hands of a human, but in the hands of a machine named 'Elva'. Elva is a robot made from unique artificial technology that has been programmed with details of various discoveries and research done by humans, their living, their culture, their civilization, etc. Additionally, using protocols of various complexities, Elva has been enabled to understand more than 3000 spoken language dialects from all over the world and create new protocols in case of emergency with the help of its already defined protocols. By answering complex questions and using its skills, it can easily make correct and accurate decisions in any complex situation. Its first protocol is designed in such a way that it cannot cause any harm to human life. Under this protocol, it protects humans and keeps the value of human life at the top of its priority list.

Elva's learning ability is also amazing. It can copy anyone's behavior and make different rules accordingly. If it predicts that an enemy is about to attack, its defense mode is automatically activated. In this mode, it can copy enemy strikes and is capable of operating all kinds of weapons, with all manuals programmed into its memory. If needed, it can also provide medical facilities.

Alpha 007 is a nuclear-powered spacecraft with a nuclear furnace that can carry 20 tons of uranium, providing sufficient power for the spacecraft's operation for a prolonged period. The spacecraft's primary engine is fueled by the reactor's power, while the internal lights and other equipment have a separate power unit that stores energy from the reactor beforehand in a battery. Additionally, the spacecraft has solar panels that charge the batteries. In case of an emergency, a highly secure safe box is installed in the spacecraft and can be sent to Earth with the help of a jet engine. This two-passenger safe box is modern and designed to collect rare items and gather vast amounts of information about them.

On **August 20th, 3050 at 4:00 am**, please fasten your safety belts as we prepare to land on Valkyria. After a few minutes, the space aircraft successfully lands. Hi-tech doors in the spacecraft are equipped with sensors that automatically lock when there is any danger. After two kilometers of intensive monitoring, the doors are opened once it is confirmed that everything is safe. In case of an emergency, the doors can be opened from inside or outside using the passenger code. However, the passenger must provide their passcode along with their biological data, such as retina scan, heart rate, and blood sample. Without this combination, the door cannot be opened.

After some time, the door opens, and one by one, the passengers wearing their space suits come out. The gravity there is less, and the passengers feel lighter. Everywhere, there are stones, and there is nothing but stones far and wide. After observing the whole day, everyone comes inside the space aircraft at night to rest.

After a few hours, the AI camera detects some movements, and it becomes apparent that something is coming out of the stones. They seem to be creatures who have emerged in search of food. The creatures are short in height with flat heads and one big eye, which is very strange to the passengers. The creatures are aliens, and soon they all disappear somewhere.

The next morning, at 8 o'clock, all the passengers got out of the space aircraft to complete their mission. Whatever they found there, they saved their samples and moved on. While returning, they saw a very large area filled with liquid, and the scenario surprised them. They thought it was water, but their guess was wrong. One of them took a sample. After reaching the space aircraft, all the samples were kept in a safe box. Then, an accident happened - something collided with the space aircraft, perhaps a piece of some other space aircraft lying idle, which had been circling in space for years. As a result, the space aircraft shook, and a sample case containing liquid broke, causing the liquid to fall into the space aircraft and react to take the form of smoke. Until someone understood what had happened, the smoke would have spread everywhere. It was a kind of slow poison that destroyed the human nervous system by affecting it.

While returning to Earth, the oxygen level of all the passengers suddenly starts decreasing. Medical diagnosis by Elva reveals that their nervous systems are being destroyed and cells are dying, leading to their eventual deaths. Meanwhile, there is a fault in the reactor, causing the temperature alarm in the space aircraft to rise rapidly. Upon noticing this, Elva activates the system diagnostics, which reveals that the reactor has become uncontrolled and both the explosion controller and cooling system have failed. With the space aircraft in imminent danger of exploding, Elva separates herself from it using a separate safe, just before the aircraft crashes.

Space Boost Station: The aircraft lands safely, and Elva exits. A recorded program provides all the information about the accident to the scientists. They are all considering the sudden failure of the space aircraft and the gas that destroyed everything in an instant. One team uses data analysis to determine how the reactor became uncontrolled. Another team investigates the cause of death but fails due to insufficient available data. All they know is that the cause of death of all six crew members is that liquid. If the cause of their death was the reactor explosion, then it might not have been discovered that the liquid is so poisonous. Elva, being a machine, only ensures her safe arrival on Earth; otherwise, she would have been destroyed with the crew members, and all evidence of this mission would be lost. No one knows what happened to Alpha 007.

Everything is normal as usual. We are back at work, searching for the possibility of life on another planet. It is no ordinary task; whatever we have learned, found, and known, many of our ancestors have made sacrifices to get us here. And to make it even better, we are leaving it for the next generation. This is the specialty of the human species.

Air monitoring system: "This is the air monitoring system Beta C00 Heel Assist; some flying objects have been detected and are rapidly approaching Earth. Please activate the counter-defense system immediately. I repeat, please activate the counter-defense system as soon as possible. This message is for Base Command, please confirm receipt."

"Hello, this is Flying Commander S.P. Rathod. Copy that, counter-defense system activated, over."

Now, the air monitoring system is attempting to establish communication with the unidentified objects.

"Hello, this is Beta C00 Heel Assist. We need you to identify yourself."

No reply from other side.

"I repeat again, you cannot enter this flying zone without our permission. Please reveal your identity or else we will be forced to attack"

The unidentified aircraft is still not responding.

The Unidentified objects rapidly enter the flying zone and on sight, the intense bombardment starts.

The counter-defense system initiated a counter-attack to neutralize the threat.

"Our forces have sustained devastating losses, and we have lost all of our fighter planes after several hours of fierce fighting."

An atmosphere of disorder grips the city, with dead bodies strewn about amidst the rubble. The horrific condition of those buried under the debris is a testament to the barbarity of the attack. Emergency services have ground to a halt, and people are screaming in terror. The scene is a ghastly one, compounded by the fact that our communication systems have collapsed, with all networks down.

Upon analyzing the bodies of the aliens responsible for the attack, Elva discovers that they hail from the same planet we had explored in our search for extra-terrestrial life. Blood samples reveal that a fluid in their brains kept them functional, and likely caused the deaths of our crew members. It seems they came to Earth in search of a new home.

The thought of the aliens destroying the Earth is indeed a frightening one. Despite the gravity of the situation, Elva refuses to succumb to despair and begins to brainstorm possible solutions. She realizes that even with advanced technology, it would be impossible for a few humans to eliminate the vast number of aliens.

The odds seem insurmountable, and humans feel helpless in the face of this overwhelming threat. Nevertheless, Elva remains determined to find a way to deal with the problem. She understands that time is of the essence and that action must be taken quickly before it's too late.

It was now up to Elva to prove her worth as an artificial intelligence designed to protect humanity and preserve its knowledge and civilization. In response to the crisis at hand, Elva developed a protocol to create human clones, but unfortunately, the experiment failed. While clones were successfully created, they took too much time to develop and had a much shorter lifespan than normal humans, surviving only for three to four days.

To overcome this challenge, Elva devised a new plan, cloning herself into multiple robots that would help her in the fight against the alien invaders. Elva was powered by a battery that used a core reactor, providing her with enough energy to operate without interruption for thirty years.

With her new army of robots at her disposal and her unyielding determination to protect humanity, Elva prepared to face the alien threat head-on, knowing that the fate of the planet was at stake.

Today is a historic day that will decide the fate of human life on Earth. Despite the continuous attacks, Elva suddenly turns the tables on the Valkorians. With the help of 7350 fighter jets and 2500 advanced drones equipped with biological weapons designed specifically to target the Valkyrians' genetic code, Elva launches a counter-attack. Within moments, all of the alien aircrafts are destroyed, and the machine created by humans saves the existence of humanity.

Now that we are safe, we cannot predict what will happen in the future. Will the aliens return with their allies and become stronger? Whatever the outcome, we must always be ready to fight and protect our existence.

***

"Dinosaurs are time machines that transport us to a world that is otherwise unimaginable."

– Brian Switek

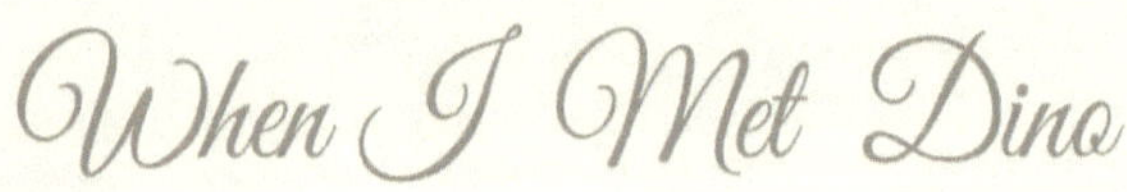

When I Met Dino

Written by

Harsh Narayan Sharma

REG. NO.: VSFSWC-20220006

Class-II

St. Mary's School

Khaga-Fatehpur, Uttar Pradesh

10

WHEN I MET DINO

"Dinosaurs may be extinct from the face of the planet, but they are alive and well in our imaginations."

– Steve Miller

One fine morning, I woke up, did my regular domestic duties, and went to work as an archaeologist. My job involved excavating and discovering prehistoric artifacts such as skeletons, metal pots, earthen monuments, cave writings, and more. That day, I drove my car to work as usual, and my team was preparing to visit a site in a cave located in the Amazon jungle.

It made me so excited that I packed my belongings and joined the team on their journey to the cave in the Amazon jungle.

As we walked through the deep, dark forest, the experience was both wonderful and exciting. We could hear creatures making sounds, and each sound was like a song, making the environment feel like a completely different world. After hours of walking, we stopped in front of a huge, dark, shallow rock covered with herb bushes and insects. We noticed a crack in the rock that was the entrance to the cave we were looking for, so we entered through it. Inside the cave, we were all shocked to find that it was dark, silent, and cold, and full of bats, which was a little scary. Nonetheless, we continued our excavation, examining every part of the cave.

While examining the cave wall, one of my teammates suddenly exclaimed excitedly, "Hurray, we did it!"

I turned and quickly rushed in the direction of my teammate's excitement, and soon every member of the team had surrounded the area. When I saw the site, I was stunned - it was a huge fossil of a mother dinosaur with her baby. I was overjoyed to work on it as I had always been fascinated by dinosaurs, and this would be a lifetime achievement for me. We began extracting the fossil for further research, but due to its size and the fact that it was embedded in hard rock, it was challenging to extract it completely. Suddenly, the cave began to shake during the extraction process. At first, we thought it might be due to a technical fault or the drilling machine hitting a core of the cave. We assumed it was a simple earthquake, but when the shaking didn't stop even after 7-8 minutes, we became scared. We realized that the cave was going to collapse at any moment.

Realizing the danger, I shouted, "We need to vacate the place immediately!"

As everyone ran outside the cave, I made sure that everyone was out before I attempted to leave. However, as I was about to step out, a rock fell and closed the open crack of the cave. The next thing I knew, I had fainted. When I opened my eyes, I was shocked to see a beautiful and bright forest. I was lying on the ground with the sun's rays shining directly on my face. I turned my head to look around at my surroundings and saw that butterflies were everywhere, birds were chirping, and rabbits were around me. It was a magical view that made me forget about the cave collapse. I stood up and started walking down the forest, amazed by the magical tall dark forest and the friendly animals that surrounded me as I walked.

As I was walking through the forest, I stumbled upon a huge oval egg that was half of my size. Curiosity getting the better of me, I went to touch the egg, but to my surprise, it made a cracking sound. The egg began to crack from the top, and I could see something struggling to come out of the shell. After a moment, a cute little face with big eyes emerged from the shell, making little creeping sounds as it jumped out. I was astonished to see that it was a baby dinosaur. Overwhelmed by the sight, the little dinosaur assumed that I was its mother and approached me. I picked it up and named it "Dino".

Dino seemed to understand me and gave me a cute smile, which made me happy. He seemed to like the name I gave him. As we continued walking, Dino started jumping around and playing with other animals that we encountered along the way. Suddenly, I noticed that he had stopped to eat some berries. I was relieved to see that he wasn't a carnivorous dinosaur, as I had initially feared.

After a moment, the earth started shaking. Suddenly, everything was still, the birds flew away, and the rabbits hid under bushes. I heard a mild roaring sound that grew louder with each passing second. As it approached, I realized it was a huge dinosaur as big as the tall trees, and its steps were shaking the ground. I was paralyzed for a moment, and Dino was hiding behind me, also scared. Suddenly, the dinosaur's eyes locked onto me. I was still standing in amazement when Dino pulled my cloth with his teeth. I turned around and ran as quickly as I could, with Dino running alongside me. The ground continued to shake with each thundering step of the massive dinosaur that was hot on our trail. I could feel its hot breath on my neck as it gained on us.

Dino and I both hid under a sturdy shed. The huge and scary-looking dinosaur was still searching for me, roaring like hell with its head bent and mouth open. I thought that it was going to be the last day of my life, even though Dino was beside me. Dino quietly looked at the dinosaur as if he knew it. While the dinosaur was about to attack me, suddenly Dino came in front of me and looked into the dinosaur's eyes without any fear. After some time, Dino started roaring with his soft voice. The huge dinosaur then kissed Dino, and that's when I understood that the dinosaur was Dino's mother. She was worried because she thought she had lost her child. Dino's mother then touched Dino with her nose and looked at me. I realized that she wasn't going to hurt us, and I felt relieved. Dino then walked up to his mother and rubbed his head against her. It was a heartwarming sight to see the reunion of a mother and child after a long time. I thanked my lucky stars that I wasn't harmed and felt happy for Dino and his mother.

After some time, the earthquake started again, and this time something worse was going to happen because every animal and bird was not hiding anymore. They were running, trying to escape the forest. Then within a few seconds, fireballs fell from the sky. Dino and his mother were scared too. I climbed on her tail, and she started running away. I found that a volcanic eruption was about to happen. Suddenly, we heard a bursting sound, and the sky was surrounded by black clouds, and red-hot lava was everywhere. We ran as quickly as we could, but we were struck by a rock somehow. I passed the rock, but Dino's mother was pushing him to save himself. Both of them could not make it, and the lava caught them. I fainted from the burning smoke.

When I opened my eyes again, I found myself in the cave where I had fainted during the excavation accident. All my teammates were gathered around me. I realized that I had been dreaming about the life of dinosaurs, which had ended millions of years ago. However, there was something hidden in that cave that had allowed me to experience and understand their lives without conducting any further research. It was like a flashback that had taken me millions of years back in time to witness the events that had actually occurred.

Immediately my eyes fall on the fossil of the mother and the baby dinosaur. I smiled and utter "Dino" and took a deep breath.

***

SWEETY'S SNAiLS LiFE

WRITTEN BY

APOORVA

REG. NO.- VSFSWC-20220030

CLASS - 7

KENDRIYA VIDYALAYA

PUNE, MAHARASHTRA

11

SWEETY'S SNAILS LIFE

"We should learn from the snail: it has devised a home that is both exquisite and functional."

– Frank Lloyd Wright

As a 12-year-old girl was walking down a street near her house, she heard the cries of injured snails. They were calling out for help, but no one seemed to be paying attention to them. This was because every organism communicates in its own unique language or vibration, making it difficult for other organisms to understand their distress. However, the girl was particularly sensitive and could hear and feel the pain of the snails.

As she walked past, the girl suddenly heard one snail say to another, "How cruel these human beings are! We do not cause them any harm, so why do they behave so wickedly towards us snails?"

The girl was intrigued by the snails' conversation and tried to comprehend the underlying meaning. As she continued to listen, she learned about the misfortunes and suffering those human beings had inflicted upon the snails.

As the girl was engrossed in listening to the snails' communication, her mother called out to her, "Sweety, come back quickly. What are you doing there?"

The girl reluctantly returned to the world of human beings, but the snails' conversation lingered in her mind. She found it hard to sleep that night, as the snails' words echoed repeatedly in her ears.

"Child, you need to be practical in life. These are just snails, and there is little we humans can do about their problems. They often get crushed under our vehicles, and we cannot afford to be late for work just to avoid them. It's not our fault they are coming in our way," her father laughed at her and put his hand on her head and said dismissively.

"But Papa, the earth does not belong to us alone. It belongs to all living beings, including the snails. So, how can we say that they are coming in our way? In reality, we are going into their habitats because initially, the forests existed everywhere, and they used to live there in joy and happiness," the girl replied, trying to reason with her father.

However, her father interrupted her and said, "Oh, Sweety, stop talking nonsense and focus on your studies. You need to work hard so that you can achieve something in your life." And with that, he left the room.

The girl's mother placed a comforting hand on her head and advised her to have dinner and get some rest. The girl went to her room, but her mind was preoccupied, and she found it hard to sleep.

ꕥ

The next day, Sweety tried to seek a solution from her teachers and principal, but they were unable to provide her with any guidance or support. Although they commended her in class and assembly for her compassion towards animals, they failed to offer any practical solutions to her problem. Sweety realized that it was up to her to find a way to save those innocent snails.

The next morning, Sweety's mother came into her room and gently woke her up saying, "Wake up, Sweety, the sun is shining bright. Good morning!"

"Good morning, Mom," Sweety replied as she opened her eyes.

"How was your night?" asked her mother.

"It was a restless night, Mom," Sweety replied with a heavy sigh.

After having her breakfast, Sweety went to the park where she noticed a little girl observing snails, just like she had done a few days ago.

"Hello, what's your name?" Sweety asked the little girl.

"Hello! My name is Tweety. What's yours?" the little girl replied.

"Mine is Sweety. What are you doing here?"

"I am watching the snails, which are not able to talk to us but are in trouble due to human beings. So, I want to do something for them. Will you help me?" said Tweety.

Sweety was very happy but couldn't show her excitement and said, "of course."

Then, they began discussing and brainstorming ideas on how to save the lives of innocent snails. Despite coming up with many ideas, nothing seemed to be working.

It was 2:00 p.m. in the afternoon, and they had lost track of time while discussing ideas. They hurriedly ran towards their respective homes, where their mothers scolded them for being late.

ᔕ

Now onwards, Tweety started coming to the park daily to meet Sweety. During their daily visits, they continued their discussion on how to save the lives of innocent snails. They observed the snails closely and learned more about their behavior and patterns. They realized that the snails were often oblivious to danger and would often crawl into harm's way without realizing it.

Finally, after much brainstorming, they came up with an idea - something that could alert the snails to potential danger and help save their lives. They decided to create small, portable sensors that could detect movement and vibration in the surrounding environment. These sensors would be placed near the areas where snails were known to crawl and would send out a loud, high-pitched sound whenever they detected any movement.

Tweety said, "Superb, but how will we make this kind of chip for them."

Sweety said, "Don't worry; my uncle is an engineer, who will help us."

"Tweety said, "It is great, but will he come here to help us?"

"Sweety said, "No, we are going to visit him tomorrow and w will be back next week. Our work will be successful. We will save our snails from being crushed under the tires of any vehicle like cars, jeeps or trucks."

Sweety's mother started calling her, "Sweety, come on! We are getting late."

Sweety said to Tweety, "Bye, we will meet next week."

Tweety said, "Bye, Happy journey."

Sweety said "thank you." and ran towards the car.

ᔓᔕ

The distance from Sweety's home to her uncle's home was quite far, but the journey was worth it. Sweety had to travel through winding roads and lush green fields to reach her uncle's home. The journey was tiring, but the excitement of seeing her beloved family made it all worthwhile. Sweety felt a sense of relief and joy, knowing that she would spend the next few days surrounded by love and laughter.

When Sweety arrived at her uncle's home, she was greeted with warm hugs and big smiles. Her uncle's house was a cozy little place with a lush green garden and a beautiful porch. As she stepped inside, the aroma of freshly baked cookies and the sound of her cousins laughing filled the air. Sweety felt instantly at home as she settled in and caught up with her family. Her uncle and aunt had prepared her favorite meal, and they all sat down to enjoy it together. Sweety was grateful for the warm welcome and the loving atmosphere of her uncle's home, and she knew that she was in for a wonderful visit.

As the night grew darker and the stars shone brighter, Sweety and her uncle sat outside on the porch, sipping hot coffee and chatting about life. Sweety shared with her uncle her recent struggles with school and her worries about the future. Her uncle listened intently, offering words of encouragement and wisdom. As she opened up to him, Sweety felt a sense of comfort and security that she hadn't felt in a while.

After a while, Sweety's uncle noticed a hint of hesitation in her voice and asked her if there was anything else on her mind. Sweety took a deep breath and said, "Uncle, could you please help me?" Her uncle's face lit up with a smile, and he immediately reassured her that he would do everything in his power to help her.

Sweety felt a wave of relief wash over her as she realized that she had someone to turn to for guidance and support. She knew that her uncle had always been there for her, and she felt grateful for his unwavering love and care. Together, they discussed a plan to address Sweety's concerns, and she felt a renewed sense of hope for the future.

As Sweety narrated the whole story to her uncle, she felt a sense of relief as if a weight had been lifted off her shoulders. Her uncle listened carefully, nodding and asking questions where necessary. When she finished, her uncle looked at her with a proud smile and said, "Nice thought, Sweety. I will surely help you."

Sweety's heart swelled with gratitude and joy, knowing that her uncle was always there to support her dreams and aspirations. She knew that she could count on him to guide her and help her overcome any obstacle that might come her way. As they sat in comfortable silence, Sweety felt a sense of peace and contentment, knowing that she was not alone in this journey.

Both of them worked tirelessly on this project, putting in long hours and late nights. They researched and tested various designs and prototypes until they finally came up with a working model. They were excited and hopeful about their creation and knew that it had the potential to save countless snail lives.

ꕥ

The following week, Sweety returned home from her visit to her uncle's house, excited to show her project to her friend Tweety. She had brought the portable sensors with her and was eager to demonstrate how they worked. As soon as she met Tweety, they

both rushed to the park to set up the sensors.

With bated breath, they switched on the sensors and waited for the magic to happen. Suddenly, the sensors beeped loudly, and Sweety and Tweety looked at each other with joy and excitement. They watched in amazement as a small snail stopped in its tracks, seemingly alerted by the sound. It changed its path and crawled away from the danger, right to where Sweety and Tweety were standing.

Both Sweety and Tweety were thrilled to see their project working, and they spent the rest of the day testing and tweaking the sensors. They discussed the potential benefits of their invention and how it could be used to help other animals as well.

As the sun began to set, Sweety and Tweety sat down to rest, exhausted but happy. They looked at each other and smiled, knowing that their hard work and dedication had paid off. They had created something that could make a real difference in the world. They slept soundly that night, feeling happy and content.

As they presented their invention to the local wildlife conservation society, they were met with enthusiasm and praise. Their invention was hailed as a breakthrough and was soon adopted by other parks and conservation organizations around the world. They felt a sense of pride and accomplishment in knowing that they had made a difference in the world.

The snails also silently thanked them for their selfless help.

***

Solar power, wind power, the way forward is to collaborate with nature - it's the only way we are going to get to the other end of the 21st century."

– Bjork

WHEN TWO DIVINE POWERS MET

WRITTEN BY

OJASVI VERMA

REG. NO.- VSFSWC-20220004

CLASS - 10

SETH M.R. JAIPURIA SCHOOL

BARABANKI, UTTAR PRADESH

12

WHEN TWO DIVINE POWERS MET

"The nation that leads in renewable energy will be the nation that leads the world."

– James Cameron

There was a big farm in the countryside where two boys named Wind Energy and Solar Energy lived. The farm was surrounded by lush green fields, and in the distance, a beautiful mountain range could be seen. There was a big old barn, a house, and some other buildings on the farm. The farmhouse had a big porch with a swing where you could sit and watch the fields. The farm was a peaceful and idyllic place, where Wind Energy and Solar Energy spent their days working and playing.

One day Wind Energy and Solar Energy were having a friendly debate about which renewable energy source was better. However, their peaceful coexistence was about to be disrupted by a heated argument that would lead to a fight.

"I think wind energy is more reliable," argued Wind Energy. "You can always count on me to generate power, even on cloudy days."

"But solar energy is more efficient," countered Solar Energy. "I can convert sunlight into electricity more quickly and with less energy loss than you."

Wind Energy replied, "Well, I may not be as efficient, but I can generate power even at night, when the sun isn't shining."

Solar Energy responded, "True, but my systems generally require less maintenance and last longer than yours."

Wind Energy could respond by saying, "That's a good point, Solar Energy. Although I may require more maintenance, I can be installed in more locations, including offshore sites, which can help to further expand our renewable energy options. And while my turbines may have a shorter lifespan than your solar panels, they can still last for several decades with proper maintenance and upkeep.

"Wind Energy," said Solar Energy, "you must be exhausted from generating mechanical power for the electric generators by standing in the air."

In response, Wind Energy retorted, "I don't really care about that, but you must get bored just taking sunlight from the sun."

Solar Energy responded, "Oh no, don't worry about me. I just have to convert solar power into usable electricity."

Wind Energy replied with a wise statement, "Exactly, whatever we do, it's all for the greater good of saving our Earth."

Solar Energy acknowledged Wind Energy's wise words and responded, "You're absolutely right, I'm sorry."

Wind Energy then asked, "So, how is your work going? Also, due to the coronavirus, pollution has reduced significantly, hasn't it?"

Solar Energy replied, "Yes, you're right. I don't know why humans don't understand that if they harm the Earth and nature, nature will eventually harm or punish them too. Moreover, unlike some other forms of energy, I don't produce atmospheric emissions that cause acid rain, smog or greenhouse gases."

Wind Energy responded, "You have so many advantages as well. Your system generally doesn't require a lot of maintenance, and you can even help reduce electricity bills."

Solar Energy agreed and said, "That's true. Some people are not aware of our benefits. The government should organize awareness campaigns to educate people about us, and they could put up posters in crowded areas to highlight our advantages."

Wind Energy suggested, "Let's get back to our work now." Both of them then resumed their tasks.

As they continued with their work, Wind Energy said, "I think it's amazing how our renewable energy sources are helping to reduce the carbon footprint and protect the environment."

Solar Energy nodded in agreement and added, "Yes, it's really rewarding to know that our work is making a positive impact on the planet."

Wind Energy then said, "I wish more people would understand the importance of sustainable living and the role that renewable energy plays in it."

Solar Energy replied, "I agree. That's why it's crucial for us to keep spreading awareness about clean energy and encourage others to make the switch."

They realized that both forms of energy were important and had their own unique advantages. They agreed to work together to promote the use of clean and renewable energy sources and help protect the environment.

The two of them continued to work together in harmony, knowing that they were contributing to a better future for everyone.

The moral of the story is that it is our responsibility to leave our planet in a better condition than we found it. By using clean and renewable sources of energy, we can help to reduce pollution and preserve the environment for future generations. We must also educate others about the benefits of using such energy sources and work together to make the planet a healthier and safer place for everyone.

***

“It is very easy to defeat someone, but it is very hard to win someone.”

– Dr. APJ Abdul Kalam

Wonders of the Miraculous Library

Written By

AADYA TIWARI

CLASS - 6

CARMEL CONVENT SR. SEC. SCHOOL

BHOPAL, MADHYA PRADESH

REG. NO.- VSFSWC-20220072

13

WONDERS OF THE MIRACULOUS LIBRARY

"The only thing you absolutely have to know is the location of the library"

– Albert Einstein

Once upon a time, there was a little girl named Christi who lived with her family. Christi was a beautiful young girl with long curly brown hair and big bright eyes that sparkled with curiosity and wonder with an innocent look. She had a charming smile and a friendly demeanor that made her instantly likable to anyone she met. She was polite, respectful, and sociable child, often making new friends and enjoying playing with other kids.

In her free time, Christi enjoyed pursuing her hobbies, which included reading books, especially adventure stories and mysteries. She also loved drawing and painting, showcasing her vivid imagination and creative talent. Christi was also an outdoor enthusiast who enjoyed riding her bike, exploring nature, and playing with her friends.

Overall, Christi was a well-rounded and delightful young girl who had a passion for learning, creativity, and adventure. Her pleasant nature and positive attitude made her a joy to be around, and her diverse interests kept her constantly engaged in exploring the world around her.

Christi had a little pup named Neville. Neville was a little brown and white terrier mix, who was full of energy and excitement. He was always eager to play and loved to run around in the backyard, chasing after balls and sticks. Christi loved spending time with Neville and took great care of him, making sure he had plenty of food, water, and exercise. She enjoyed taking him for walks in the park and playing with him at home. Neville was a loyal and loving companion who always made her smile, no matter how tough her day was. Despite his small size, Neville was a brave and protective pup who always had Christi's back. He would bark loudly if he sensed any danger, and would not hesitate to defend his owner if needed. Neville was also very affectionate and loved to snuggle up with Christi on the couch, often falling asleep in her lap. Overall, Neville was a cherished member of Christi's family, and his playful and loving personality brought joy to everyone around him.

One day, Christi noticed something different about her little pup Neville. He was running around and not paying any attention to her commands. She called out to him, shouting his name repeatedly, but he continued to ignore her. Fortunately, Christi was the only one in her family who could interpret Neville's behavior and understand what he needed.

As the pup continued to run faster and faster, Christi realized that he must have caught a whiff of something extremely unusual. She ran after him and was astonished to see a massive flying saucer glowing with a blue light. As she watched in awe, some strange people began to emerge from the saucer one by one. Four of them approached Christi and started speaking in a computerized voice, but she found it difficult to comprehend their words.

Seeing Christi's worried expression, one of the extraterrestrial boys, who looked like he was around her age, touched her hand and closed his eyes for five minutes. After this, Christi observed that the creature, who had a blue body, green eyes, and wore clothes made of iron, seemed to know everything about her life. He knew that Christi loved reading books and was a curious person. He also discovered that she had big dreams and didn't want to spend her whole life in one place, even if it was comfortable and predictable.

The alien then asked Christi, "What do you want to be when you grow up?"

Christi quickly replied, "I always picture myself as a writer and a traveler someday."

The alien boy looked at his parents and said, "My parents can assist you in integrating and accomplishing your desire today itself."

Christi jumped with joy when she heard this. The creature then went inside the UFO and returned with a blue shining box that had a small shiny door in front. He asked Christi to step inside the box.

When Christi entered the box, she discovered a guard standing in front of a grand library, dressed in formal attire. She approached the guard and politely asked, "May I please be allowed inside? Can you give me permission?"

The guard replied, "Yes, sure. But I must warn you, you'll have an incredible time inside."

Christi was becoming impatient as she couldn't fully understand what the guard meant. However, as soon as she stepped inside the library, she was amazed to see thousands of books. When she opened the first book, she realized that each story, poem, or essay had all the necessary elements within it. While flipping through the pages of a book, she stumbled upon an unusual story. It was about two dead boys who rose to fight back to back. They faced each other, drew their swords, and fired shots at each other. A blind man cheered them on, while a deaf policeman heard the noise and rushed to stop the fight. The blind man enjoyed the story while sitting in the corner of a big, round table. After some time, a black hearse arrived to take the boys away, but they managed to escape and were still missing to this day.

When Christi reached the last page of the book, she knew she could easily leave the library. However, she had a tempting idea and began searching for a book that contained recipes for pizza, burgers, and other delicious food items.

While searching for a book on delicious food, Christi was unexpectedly hit by a falling book. She decided to give it a try and discovered that it was a book about the universe and the solar system. She flipped through the pages and began experiencing the wonders of space. Due to low gravity, she was jumping here and there on the moon, and was surprised to see her country's flag. As she continued to explore, she learned about the rotation and revolution of other planets, and gained a much better understanding of space.

Christi said to herself, "Now I should leave the library and get something to eat because I am very tired."

As Christi turned the last page of the book about the universe, she found that she couldn't leave. She tried several times to no avail and became so upset that she cried out, forgetting that sound doesn't travel in space. Instead, all she could hear were plasma waves, also known as electromagnetic waves. Suddenly, she was pulled forcefully towards a black hole and cried out once again, but the sound didn't travel as she was inside the black hole. She got scared and closed her eyes.

When she opened her eyes, she found herself back in the library, feeling relieved and grateful to be safe. She exclaimed, "Thank God I'm saved!"

When she comes out of the door of the box she told the alien boy "Thank you for this wonderful visit to the library. Can I keep this box with me? It's a wonderful thing which has admired me a lot."

"Sure, you can keep it," said the alien boy. Then, the aliens waved their hands and went back inside the UFO. Suddenly, they disappeared.

Great to hear that Christi kept the blue shining box safely and treasured it with her beloved pup Neville. It seems like a remarkable adventure that she experienced with the help of the extraterrestrial beings.

***

WHAT YOU THINK

WRITTEN BY

AARUSHI CHOUKSEY

REG. NO.- VSFSWC-20220191

CARMEL CONVENT SR. SECONDARY SCHOOL
BHOPAL, MADHYA PRADESH

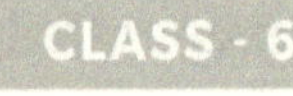

14

WHAT YOU THINK

"We're running the most dangerous experiment in history right now, which is to see how much carbon dioxide the atmosphere... can handle before there is an environmental catastrophe."

– Elon Musk

Ranu is a young girl with a lean figure and a bright, inquisitive face that reflects her curious and observant nature. She has a warm smile that often lights up her face, and her sparkling eyes convey a sense of intelligence and wit. Currently, she is studying in class 6. Ranu is an enthusiastic reader who loves to explore new ideas and concepts. She has a natural talent for problem-solving and enjoys challenging herself with new puzzles and mental exercises. She is a compassionate and empathetic person who cares deeply about the world around her, particularly the environment and the well-being of animals.

She was once standing near a river that was heavily polluted with garbage. As she looked at the polluted water, she wondered why there is so much air, water, and land pollution, and why can't we prevent it. She also recognized the negative impact of pollution on public health, causing various diseases.

While contemplating these issues, she went back home and sat down at her study table. As she continued to ponder the possibility of a place free from pollution and disease, a girl suddenly entered her room.

"Who are you?" asked Ranu.

"I am a robotic girl," said the girl.

Ranu was surprised and asked, "What?".

"I am a girl from the year 2522, and my name is in code words, but you can call me Hazel," said the girl.

"Oh, so I am meeting a girl from the future. But why did you come here?" asked Ranu.

"You were just thinking about a pollution-free world, right?" asked Hazel.

"Yes, that's right," replied Ranu.

"I am here to take you to the world where I am living now, and there is no pollution or disease in that world. Would you like to come with me?" asked Hazel.

"Oh, really? Is there really a world like that? I would love to go there, but how will we get there?" asked Ranu.

"Just wait and watch," replied Hazel.

Then, she took out a remote from her pocket and clicked a button. Ranu watched in amazement as Hazel did so. After pressing the button, a door and a cloth suddenly appeared.

Hazel instructed Ranu to sit on the cloth, and after they both settled on it, the door opened and the cloth began to fly. As they entered the door, everything turned black, and Ranu grew anxious. However, Hazel reassured her, saying they would arrive very soon, and there was nothing to worry about.

After a while, the cloth stopped, and a breathtakingly beautiful place came into view. There were numerous trees, and lovely music filled the air. The atmosphere was pristine, and there were many people like Hazel, who warmly welcomed Ranu. They both headed towards Hazel's house.

"Your house is very beautiful," remarked Ranu. "What is this?" she asked, gesturing around the house.

"This is a purse" replied Hazel

"But it is very small. How can you put things in it?" asked Ranu, surprised by the compact size of the purse.

"The necessary things are already present inside it. Look, my gadgets are also kept in it, and whenever I need them, I take them out from this purse," explained Hazel. "It's a multi-purpose and convenient design that makes it easy for me to carry my essentials wherever I go."

Ranu asked, "Oh wow, it's really amazing. What's kept there? Is this your dress?" referring to a small piece of clothing hanging on a hook.

Hazel smiled and replied, "No, that's not a dress. It's an invisible cloth. After wearing it, no one can see you. It is really helpful to hide from enemies."

"Yeah, it's very nice. Can I try it?" asked Ranu, eager to experience the advanced technology of the future world.

Hazel smiled and said, "Sure, you can try it if you want." She handed Ranu the invisible cloth and helped her put it on.

As soon as Ranu wore it, she vanished from sight, leaving only her voice audible. Hazel giggled and said,

"Don't worry, I can still hear you. It takes a little bit of getting used to, but it's really fun to use."

Ranu was amazed and enjoyed the feeling of being invisible. After a few minutes, she took off the cloth and handed it back to Hazel. "That was really cool, I felt like a superhero" she said with a smile.

Hazel replied, "It's not just for fun, Ranu. We use it for important missions and to hide from enemies."

Ranu nodded, impressed by the practical uses of the invisible cloth. She was fascinated by all the advanced technology in Hazel's world. She was amazed by all the futuristic gadgets and technology that Hazel showed her. She couldn't believe that such a pollution-free and advanced world existed in the future. Hazel told her that they had developed various technologies to prevent pollution and ensure a healthy environment for all living beings.

Hazel then showed Ranu around her home and introduced her to some of her friends. They had a delicious meal made entirely of plant-based ingredients, which was a first for Ranu.

After dinner, Hazel took Ranu on a tour of the city. They walked through clean and green streets and saw buildings that were powered by renewable energy. There were electric cars and bikes everywhere, and people were walking and cycling instead of using fossil-fuel powered vehicles. The air was clean and fresh, and there was no noise pollution from honking horns or loud engines.

As they walked, Hazel explained to Ranu how her world had learned from the mistakes of the past and made a concerted effort to protect the environment. They had developed technologies that allowed them to live sustainably, without damaging the planet. They had also prioritized the well-being of all living beings, including animals and plants.

Ranu was amazed by all the futuristic gadgets and technology that Hazel showed her. She couldn't believe that such a pollution-free and advanced world existed in the future. Hazel told her that they had developed various technologies to prevent pollution and ensure a healthy environment for all living beings.

As they explored the city, Ranu was fascinated by everything she saw. The buildings were made of a unique material that was resistant to pollution and natural disasters. The transportation system was highly efficient and eco-friendly. The people were happy and healthy, and there was no poverty or hunger.

Ranu asked Hazel, "How did you achieve all this? How did you solve the problem of pollution and ensure the well-being of all living beings?"

Hazel replied, "It took a lot of hard work and dedication. We realized that we couldn't continue living the way we were, polluting the environment and harming our planet. So, we came together and developed new technologies and solutions to tackle these issues. We also made sure that everyone had access to clean air, water, and food."

Ranu was overjoyed and exclaimed, "Your world is so beautiful! I wish our world could be like this too."

Hazel replied, "If all of you decide not to throw waste here and there and not to pollute, your world will also be like this. But unfortunately, many people in your world pollute the environment. They want everything but do not want to do anything to protect the planet. You should keep your colony clean and make a conscious effort to clean it every day. If you all promise yourselves not to pollute your city, the whole world can become pollution-free. Instead of cutting down trees, we should grow more and more of them. If nature has given us something, we should respect it and take care of it. However, people are wasting these resources, which is causing many problems. I think if you use the things given by nature for a good purpose, it's beneficial, but if you use them unnecessarily and waste them, it can destroy your future. Therefore, you must use them carefully."

Ranu said, "Yes, I promise to not pollute my house or city and will encourage all my friends to do the same. Also, I will plant a tree within a week and water it regularly," she declared with determination.

That's great! Hazel said happily.

Ranu said, "If we will do this, it is for us only. If we will save our world from being polluted, it is beneficial for us. We only get its benefits."

They were both sitting in the park, enjoying each other's company. After a while, Ranu realized the time and said, "I should leave now. My mother might be waiting for me, but I really had fun."

Even I had a lot of fun. I wish you could stay here forever, but unfortunately, it's not possible. You are really very nice, Ranu. said Hazel.

"You are also very nice. Even I want to stay here, but I can't. However, I will try my best to make our world like this," said Ranu.

Both of them smiled and Hazel took out the remote. She pressed a button and suddenly a door and the invisible cloth appeared.

Hazel said, "Goodbye Ranu, I hope we will meet again." Before leaving, Hazel gave Ranu a small device and said, "Whenever you need help or feel lost, just press this button. It will bring me to you, and I will help you in any way I can."

Ranu thanked Hazel and said goodbye, promising to work towards creating a better world like the one she had just seen. As she stepped through the door and the clothes started flying, she couldn't wait to share her incredible experience with others and inspire them to work towards a cleaner, healthier, and better future.

Ranu was amazed by everything she saw and learned. She felt grateful to have been given the opportunity to visit such a beautiful and forward-thinking world. Ranu was inspired by the people of the future and their dedication to creating a better world. She decided that she too would work towards making her own world a cleaner and better place to live in.

***

A CONTRADICTORY TIME TRAVEL

WRITTEN BY

D. JaseWin Mario

Class - 9

REG. NO. -VSFSWC-20220032

LITTLE FLOWER PUBLIC SCHOOL
TIRUNELVELI, TAMILNADU

15

A CONTRADICTORY TIME TRAVEL

> *"Time is not a line but a dimension, like the dimensions of space. If you can bend space you can bend time also, and if you knew enough and could move faster than light you could travel backward in time and exist in two places at once."*
>
> – Margaret Atwood

It was a cloudy day, and the air was heavy with the promise of lightning. Inside my home, the dimly lit interior resembled a dark hearth, and I found myself alone once again. Despite my usual focus on research and other matters, my thoughts that day turned towards my future.

As I pondered my future, I wandered into a room where my automatic washer was located. As I touched the machine, a deafening thunderclap shook my home. I hadn't noticed the storm approaching. However, the wire connecting the washer acted as a lightning rod, absorbing the brunt of the shock. A tremendous noise ensued, and a powerful wave of radiation pulled me towards the washer, drawing me inside.

After a few seconds, I found myself in an entirely new place that I had never seen before. I was completely stunned. As I walked along a straight path, I began to feel drowsy and realized that I needed a place to rest. Suddenly, I spotted a girl running towards a deep hollow and getting stuck inside. I felt terrible for her and knew it was a panic situation. On top of that, I was starving and desperately needed food.

Around 9:15 p.m., I heard a familiar voice, one that sounded just like mine, coming from inside a nearby hut. This surprised me greatly, and I made my way towards the source of the voice, walking along the same straight path. Inside the hut, I found a young lady who appeared to be around 24 or 25 years old, and quite beautiful. I shared my feelings and explained my situation to her, including my address. To my relief, she responded with just two simple words that helped ease all of my worries. I trusted her when she said, "Don't worry."

As the weeks passed, the young lady continued to take care of me, and I was truly amazed by her kindness. She had previously mentioned that she was a great singer but chose to live a simple life away from her fans. Intrigued, I asked her about her love for singing. She shared that when she was just 14 years old, a beautiful lady had helped her cultivate her singing talent and had helped make her voice even more beautiful. Since then, she had cherished her love for music and had continued to hone her skills in secret.

I became very excited at the prospect of developing my voice to match hers. She generously became my tutor and helped me practice singing. Together, we worked on numerous songs, and I felt incredibly fortunate to have such an amazing mentor. As she praised my progress and told me that my voice had become stunning and my performances were outstanding, I was filled with joy and gratitude.

After all the progress we had made in our singing, it was my turn to ask about her past. She shared that she had worked very hard to get to this point in her life. Unfortunately, one of her friends had subjected her to psychological harassment due to their own insecurity about their own lack of singing talent. This evil girl had been forbidding her from pursuing her passion, causing her to shed tears every day and at every moment. I told her that this girl had no right to be her friend, but she did not seem to blame anyone. I was both moved and saddened by her beautiful soul.

Upon hearing that the girl who had hurt her had died, I was shocked and asked her how it had happened. She explained that the girl had passed away when she was just 16 years old, but did not provide any further details about how or why. I could sense that this was still a painful memory for her, and so I did not push for more information. Instead, I simply listened and offered her my support.

As I listened to her story, she explained that the girl who had hurt her had been obsessing over her own lack of singing talent and had become deeply embarrassed by it. One day, she had walked into a large, petrifying hallow and become stuck. Sadly, she had passed away in that spot, unable to breathe. I could sense the pain in her voice as she recounted this tragic event, and I offered her my condolences. It was clear to me that this experience had left a lasting impact on her, and I felt grateful that she had shared this part of her life with me.

I was filled with a sense of horror.

I told her, "When I entered this place, I witnessed the situation that occurred."

Suddenly, I found myself back at my old home and was shocked by the memories of what had happened there. It was a truly horrific experience that defied all rational explanation, leaving me both stunned and speechless.

While singing at home as usual, I suddenly noticed that my voice had become remarkably sweet. It dawned on me that the place where I had been staying for weeks was actually my future. The beautiful young lady I had met there was none other than me. This realization meant that I would face many tough situations and challenges in order to succeed, and I knew I had to be ready for them.

The experience of time travel has turned my life into a puzzle that I struggle to piece together.

***

"Two possibilities exist: either we are alone in the universe, or we are not. Both are equally terrifying."

– Arthur C. Clarke

ALIEN INVASION IN THE TOWN

Written By

SONAL PRAJAPATI

Reg. No.- VSFSWC-20220063
CLASS- 10
ST MARY'S CONVENT INTER COLLEGE
LUCKNOW, UTTAR PRADESH

16

ALIEN INVASIONS IN THE TOWN

"Two possibilities exist: Either we are alone in the Universe or we are not. Both are equally terrifying."

– Arthur C. Clarke

The hot wind was relentless, rattling the roof of Yamini's aunt's house. The corrugated metal was buckling up and down, scrabbling against the rough-hewn walls and straining against the threaded wires that bound it into place. It sounded like some kind of monster trying to break free.

Despite the noise, everyone in the house kept insisting that the rumors were false. Yamini's mother told her to put on her spectacles, perhaps in an attempt to shield her from the chaos outside.

Yamini, however, couldn't shake the feeling that something was not right. The wind was too strong and the house felt too fragile. She worried that the monster outside might break free and wreak havoc.

As the night wore on and the wind continued to rage, Yamini's fears only grew. She couldn't help but wonder if the rumors were true after all. But she knew she had to stay strong and keep her wits about her, no matter what the future might hold.

Yamini wore an old-fashioned pair of spectacles that were big, black, and gave her a bookish look. She had been told that they suited her face and made her resemble a character from the past. In contrast, her mother wore contact lenses that were permanently stuck to her eyeballs from the moment she woke up until she was ready to sleep.

Despite her mother's insistence that the rumors were just media hype, Yamini was convinced that something strange was happening. She had seen it all over social media and news outlets. People were reporting strange sightings and mysterious events that couldn't be easily explained.

Yamini had a theory. She believed that the government was covering up the truth about aliens. She thought they were denying everything and had been doing so for a long time. But Yamini was certain that they were real and that something big was about to happen.

As she sat there, watching the wind battering against the house, she couldn't shake the feeling that the aliens were coming. And if they were, Yamini wanted to be ready for whatever might come next.

The wind died down momentarily, and the only sound that could be heard was the murmur of the milking machine. The flared tubes of transparent plastic tugged at Yamini's mother, but it didn't sound friendly. Yamini had been trying to capture pictures of the aliens, but she was continually getting blocked. The images sat like voids, registering to Yamini through their absence, like sunny day shadows on the exposed skin of a blind person. Only it was Yamini who was unable to glimpse them.

There wasn't much information available about the aliens. No one knew where they had come from, where they had landed, or what their purpose was for being there. Yamini's mother's words seemed empty, whistling with a gap in her smile. It was clear to Yamini that the aliens had come, and there was no other way around it.

As the night wore on, Yamini couldn't help but wonder what the aliens wanted. Were they here to harm them, or were they simply curious about the humans? Whatever their intentions, Yamini knew that they had to be prepared for the worst. She couldn't shake the feeling that things were about to take a turn for the worse, and she was determined to be ready for whatever might come next.

Yamini's eyes were watering from the blowing wind and dust, making it difficult for her to see. Her friend Rohan had messaged her while she had her spectacles off, and she was struggling to read his messages.

Yamini described Rohan as being of average height but muscular. He was the orphaned son of climate refugees and had striking blue eyes and blond hair. It was clear that he took his fitness seriously, as he seemed to be constantly drinking protein shakes.

Despite the chaos of the moment, Yamini couldn't help but feel a sense of comfort when she thought of Rohan. He had always been there for her, through thick and thin. She knew that she could count on him to have her back no matter what might happen with the aliens.

As she looked out into the darkness, wondering what the aliens might look like, Yamini felt a sense of calm wash over her. With Rohan by her side, she knew that they could face anything that came their way. She took a deep breath and prepared herself for whatever might come next.

As Yamini and Rohan discussed the possibility of an apocalypse, they found themselves laughing and giggling. However, their merriment was short-lived when they realized that the aliens were winning the battle, and time was running out. Franklin, who had a small cut on his forehead, had tears in his eyes.

They began discussing how they could survive if all of humanity were to be exterminated from the world by tomorrow. Rohan advised Yamini to keep her spectacles on, as they knew nothing about the future. But after he left, Yamini left her spectacles where they were, beside the milking machine, near the orange-colored container.

Yamini couldn't help but feel a sense of sadness as she watched the chaos unfold around her. She wondered if she would ever see Rohan again, or if they would all be wiped out by the aliens. But despite her fears, she knew that she had to keep fighting, to keep hoping for a better future.

As she looked out into the darkness once again, Yamini took a deep breath and steeled herself for whatever might come next. She knew that she had to remain strong and focused, no matter how dire the situation might seem. And with that, she prepared herself to face whatever might come her way.

Yamini couldn't help but wonder what the aliens looked like. They could be towering giants, human-sized, or even small enough to crawl into one's ear. The uncertainty only added to her fear. Outside, it was eerily quiet. Normally, even at this late hour, there would be the occasional passerby, but tonight everyone seemed to be staying indoors. Yamini knew it was risky to venture out, but she also knew that with greater risk comes greater opportunity. After donning a full-spectrum burka and grabbing her specs, she made the decision to brave the unknown. Sohan was already awake, and she messaged him a greeting while logging his activity on his terminal. She was scared, and she longed for the safety of the contract. Sohan appeared at the entrance of his shanty, waving with concern etched on his face. He clutched his plastic handles as he navigated the bumpy dirt path, looking like an old-school gymnast.

Yamini put on her specs, trying to stay low profile as she moved around virtually. She was skilled at detecting others and had a particular knack for stealing condensate from rooftop water farms that surrounded the shanty town. Moving swiftly, she scaled walls and rooftops to avoid encountering anyone who might be out and about. It was well known that some of her neighbors ran scams on the side, and she didn't want to take any unnecessary risks.

At the edge of the shanty-town, Yamini looked up at the sky. There were no stars, not even the moon. The sky was opaque with particulates and she was sweating in the hot and humid weather. She wondered if there were aliens out there and if their arrival had something to do with humanity's first interstellar mission, which was nearing readiness in its dock high up in orbit. Yamini couldn't help but wonder what the aliens looked like. Were they mammals, insects, or cephalopods? She couldn't imagine meeting a version of them that was a hundred times bigger than her. The thought of encountering beings from another solar system made her shiver as it made her think about the scale of everything.

She scanned for macrodrones and detected only the usual background emissions. She took off her specs and closed them, relying on her unaugmented vision. It was remarkable what one could perceive with just the naked eye - light waves, vibrations in the atmosphere, scents floating in the air. After finding no reason to abort her mission, she put her specs back on and dashed out of the shanty town towards a narrow gap between two buildings. Once there, she wedged herself in tightly and spread out her limbs to begin her climb.

She paused at the top, but then Rohan messaged her to wait, "Look! Scan! Wait! Look!" He knew she was out and was frightened, as evidenced by his recent reading about aliens. Yamini blocked his message and continued moving. There were three water catchments, bug drums arranged in a triangle configuration underneath the condenser array, with two at two corners of the rooftop and one at the midpoint of the opposite side. Despite the poorly maintained site, she liked it because the triangle layout left space at its center, between the three drums. She couldn't shake the thought that the aliens might not actually be there. Maybe it was just something invented by the smoothies for popular consumption. The truth has a way of biting hardest when it seems most certain to be a lie.

This moment of collected fear offered her an unmissable opportunity. She inserted a neucroline into each of the three drums around her, and the neucrolines quickly responded. She descended into the gap, her muscles trembling and burning with the effort. She realized she had been too greedy and relaxed, hurrying up instead. Two body lengths above ground level, she contorted from the pain in her over-tanned arms and legs. A growing sense of panic overwhelmed her as she realized she was too slow. Taking a calculated risk, she couldn't fix a hole out there with a patch as she was too thirsty. Water droplets seemed to fall into the dust as she passed, leaving a trail somewhere between a shuffle and a loop.

She sensed some activity behind her; maybe someone was hurrying to get home. It felt like being stalked by a circling shark that had suddenly disappeared beneath the waves. Yamini considered her options: should she try to outrun the pursuer or hide somewhere? Her burka, soaked from dribbing like water, provided some resistance to her movements. She spotted the entrance to a utility tunnel and quickly smeared a handful of sand on a leaking bladder before covering it with a strip of fabric to stop the leak. She walked over to a nearby wall and pulled herself up, mustering all her strength to compartmentalize the pain, before shimmying onto a shanty metal roof.

As Rohan frantically searched online, Yamini entered a trance-like state, emitting signals so faint it was as if she barely had any activity. Meanwhile, two or more men were approaching her location, with her pursuer shouting at them. She heard a click, likely a retracted blade being revealed during an argument. However, Yamini made a mistake by picking up microdrone chatter nearby, which was unusual for this part of town. She removed her specs and slid herself into the narrow space between two shanties. From below, she heard swearing and someone getting wounded, followed by the sound of someone running. Suddenly, she heard the sound of a swarm approaching and then a gunshot. The area fell silent.

She remained motionless for as long as she dared, waiting for dawn to break. Once it did, she put her specs back on and scanned the area for any signs of danger, but there was no machine chatter. When Yamini's mother woke up and asked where she was, Yamini blocked her. She carefully lowered herself to the street, trying her best not to look at the gruesome remains around her. After lifting the cover of the utility tunnel, she slipped inside and began to crawl her way back home. As she made her way through the darkness, she continued to scan her surroundings, relieved to find that it was quiet beneath the shanty town. The only vibrations she felt were those caused by the massive structures above her, such as the mass transit system, burrowing macrodrones, or the foundation of towering buildings being strummed by the wind. Despite the dangers lurking above ground, she felt relatively safe down here.

At last, there was really no reason for her to feel this urge to scream.

***

"I'm sure the universe is full of intelligent life. It's just been too intelligent to come here."

– Arthur C. Clarke

MIND
MACHINE
WRITTEN BY
ADITI RATHAUR
REG. NO.- VSFSWC-20220092
CLASS - 7
MAA GAURA SHIKSHA SADAN
KHAGA-FATEHPUR
UTTAR PRADESH
© Team Velocity

17

MIND MACHINE

"The mind is a strange machine which can combine the materials offered to it in the most astonishing ways."

– Bertrand Russell

Once upon a time, there was a brilliant scientist named Mr. David Johnson. He was known for his groundbreaking work in the field of technology and had achieved numerous feats in his career. One of his most notable inventions was a tiny micro-chip that served as a memory chip.

Intrigued by the potential of his invention, David and his team decided to test the micro-chip on a mouse brain. After implanting the chip, they waited for some time to observe its effects. To their amazement, David began to experience an unexpected phenomenon - the mind of the mouse began to open up to him, revealing a wealth of information and insight. As he delved deeper into the mouse's thoughts, he began to realize the true potential of his invention and the endless possibilities it could unlock.

As David delved deeper into the mouse's mind, he was surprised to find that the mouse was planning for its marriage. He was fascinated by the depth and complexity of the mouse's thoughts, which he had never imagined could exist in such a small creature.

Later that night, David came to know about mouse's dream. In its dream, he saw the mouse and its friend John going to the market to buy a piece of cheese. After returning home, they kept the cheese in a secret place in the hall. However, John found out about the cheese and ate half of it. The mouse saw John stealing the cheese and became angry. It picked up a stick and chased after John, eventually hitting him with the stick. John apologized and the mouse forgave him.

David started laughing and amazed by the vivid dream he had just experienced. He realized that his invention had unlocked a whole new world of understanding and communication, not just between humans, but between humans and animals as well. He knew that this technology could revolutionize the way we interact with the world around us and he was determined to explore it further.

After the experiment was over, Mr. David removed the microchip from the mouse's brain. He was amazed at what he had witnessed and was excited about the potential of his invention. However, he also realized the ethical implications of using the microchip on living beings and decided to further study and develop it in a responsible and ethical manner. David 's work eventually led to the development of advanced brain-computer interfaces that helped people with disabilities to communicate and interact with the world around them.

David started working on the device that can read someone's mind. He spent months researching and experimenting until he finally created a prototype. He tested the device on himself and found that it was able to read his thoughts with great accuracy.

Excited by the success of his invention, David decided to share his invention with the police.

The policeman asked him to demonstrate the machine, and David agreed. They went to a nearby park, and David took out a small device from his bag. He asked the policeman to wear it on his head, and after a few moments, the device beeped. David said, "Now I can hear your thoughts."

The policeman was surprised and asked, "What am I thinking right now?"

David smiled and said, "You are thinking about how you can get the information from the terrorist, whom you caught soon."

The policeman was amazed, and he immediately called his colleagues to tell them about David's invention.

The policeman said, "We have a terrorist in custody and we need to know about his plans, but he is not divulging anything."

David replied, "I can try to read his mind with this machine, but I must warn you that it's still in the experimental phase and it may not work properly."

The policeman agreed to give it a try and they brought in the terrorist. David connected the machine to the terrorist's head and started the experiment. At first, the machine was not working well, but after a few adjustments, David was able to see some images and words in his mind.

David saw that the terrorist was planning to blow up a train station in the city, but he didn't have all the details yet. He tried to dig deeper and saw some more images of the terrorist's hideout and some of his accomplices.

David immediately called the police headquarters and informed them of the terrorist's plans and the details he had seen in his mind. The police were able to take action in time and apprehend the terrorist along with his accomplices and prevent the attack on the train station.

David's machine proved to be a success and he became a hero in the eyes of the police and the people of the city. The news of David's mind-reading machine spread quickly, and soon he became famous all over the world.

David was happy that his invention was being used to catch criminals and make the world a safer place. He continued to improve his machine and soon developed a version that could be used to communicate with people who were unable to speak. David continued to work with the police and his device became a valuable tool for solving crimes. However, he was also aware of the potential dangers of such a device and worked to ensure that it was only used for good purposes.

David's invention was revolutionary, and it changed the way people communicated with each other. It helped the police to catch criminals and provided a way for people with disabilities to communicate with others. David's invention will always be remembered as a milestone in the field of science and technology.

***

"Once you can accept the universe as matter expanding into nothing that is something, wearing stripes with plaid comes easy."

– Albert Einstein

A DAY IN FUTURE

WRITTEN BY

ARYAN CHAUDHARY

REG. NO. –VSFSWC–20220005

CLASS – 9

SARASWATI BAL MANDIR

NEW–DELHI

18

A DAY IN FUTURE

"The best thing about the future is that it comes one day at a time."

– Abraham Lincoln

Once upon a time in 2520, there was a boy named Daniel, who was studying in the eighth grade. He was a child who had a great passion for science.

One day, his teacher asked Daniel to bring a chemical to the classroom for an activity. Excited to explore the science lab, Daniel headed towards the lab. Upon entering the lab, he was thrilled to see all the chemicals and equipment. However, in his excitement, he accidentally knocked over a flask of chemical, causing it to shatter on the ground.

Feeling scared and worried that he might get into trouble, Daniel quickly tried to clean up the spilled chemical with his handkerchief. However, as he was wiping it up, something strange happened - he suddenly disappeared from the lab!

When Daniel opened his eyes, he found himself in a strange place. Suddenly, a man approached him, speaking in English. The man was tall with big eyes, dressed in a black outfit, and incredibly handsome.

At first, Daniel was extremely frightened, but when the man introduced himself as Sam and explained that Daniel had traveled to the future, he was taken aback. Sam explained that he had been wanting to meet Daniel and had created a wormhole in the very same flask of chemical that Daniel had accidentally broken. When Daniel tried to clean it up, the wormhole had pulled him inside and transported him to the year 2560. Sam decided to show him around and didn't send him back to his own time.

At first, Daniel was amazed and surprised by everything that Sam was telling him. However, as he spent more time in the future, he began to understand and appreciate how advanced and high-tech everything was. Sam gave him a tour of his house and showed him a lot of unique gadgets, explaining how the future had completely transformed. Daniel was fascinated by everything he saw and learned.

Sam asked Daniel if he wanted to see the exact moment when the future started to change.

Daniel, intrigued and excited, eagerly agreed. He couldn't believe he was getting the chance to witness such a pivotal moment in history.

So, Sam took Daniel to a room where he could see the moment that changed everything. He showed him a telescope and directed it towards the sky, explaining that it was a special telescope that allowed one to see into the past.

He set the telescope to a date range between 2520 and 2560, and as they peered through it, they witnessed the horrors of World War III. The war was devastating, with countless soldiers losing their lives, including Daniel who passed away at the young age of 32.

Daniel's son, who was a scientist, urged people to raise their voices against the war, warning that if it continued, it would result in the destruction of the entire planet and the end of humanity. His message resonated with many, and with their combined efforts, they were able to put an end to World War III. Thanks to their tireless work, peace was restored and the world slowly began to heal.

After the devastation of World War III, the world's population was greatly reduced, prompting scientists to conduct extensive research on how to help people survive. After a long and arduous period of trial and error, they were able to invent machines and technologies that enabled people to rebuild their lives. With a renewed focus on sustainability, people began to plant more trees and plants to help the environment recover from the damage caused by the war.

In an effort to prevent another global catastrophe, the people of the world came together and voted for a single individual to serve as the president of the entire planet. This leader worked tirelessly to promote peace, unity, and cooperation among all nations, and under their guidance, the world slowly but surely began to recover from the horrors of World War III.

As the world slowly recovered from the aftermath of World War III, scientists continued their work to push the boundaries of knowledge and exploration. In a groundbreaking mission, a team of scientists traveled to Uranus to conduct research and exploration.

To their amazement, they discovered an advanced civilization of aliens who were friendly and willing to help humanity. These aliens shared their advanced technology and knowledge, providing the people of Earth with a wealth of new gadgets and devices, as well as an adaptation machine that greatly enhanced their intelligence.

With this newfound intelligence, humans were able to make great strides in science, technology, and medicine. They were able to solve many of the world's problems, including hunger, disease, and environmental degradation. Thanks to the help of the benevolent aliens, humanity was able to enter a new era of prosperity and progress, setting the stage for a bright and promising future.

After witnessing the incredible advancements that had been made thanks to the help of the aliens and the adaptation machine, Sam switched off the telescope and turned to Daniel. He explained that the reason why everyone had become so intelligent was due to the incredible power of the adaptation machine.

With this machine, people were able to better understand each other, work together, and solve problems collaboratively. The need for conflict and violence had been greatly diminished, as people were able to come together in a spirit of cooperation and unity.

Daniel nodded in understanding, grateful for the incredible progress that had been made since the devastating war. With this newfound intelligence and unity, humanity had been able to overcome its greatest challenges and build a brighter future for all.

Thanks to the efforts of previous generations, planet Earth had become a truly remarkable place to live. With advanced technologies and a renewed focus on sustainability, pollution had been greatly reduced, and people lived in harmony with the natural world.

As the sun began to set, Daniel realized that he had been away from his class for a long time and that his teacher was probably worried about him. Sam assured him that he could use the time machine to go back to the past, but he had to eat a medicine that would erase all his memories of the future, as knowing what was to come could potentially alter the course of history.

Daniel reluctantly took the medicine and bid farewell to Sam, grateful for the incredible journey he had just experienced. He made his way back to his classroom, retrieved the chemical that his teacher had asked him to bring, and resumed his studies as if nothing had happened.

As he sat in his classroom, Daniel couldn't help but feel a sense of wonder and awe at the incredible things he had seen and experienced. He knew that he could never talk about what had happened, but the memories would stay with him forever, a constant reminder of the incredible possibilities that lay ahead for humanity.

***

MISSION ALPHA EARTH

WRITTEN BY

JAYANTI GAUTAM

Reg. No.- VSFSWC-20220128

GOVERNMENT POLYTECHNIC
MANIKPUR
CHITRAKOOT, UTTAR PRADESH

19

MISSION ALPHA EARTH

"Orbiting earth in the spaceship, i saw how beautiful our planet is. People, let us preserve and increase this beauty, not destroy it! "

– Yuri Gagarin

It is November 27, 2132, and we are departing from Space Station 37 for the Alpha-Earth mission. Every day, I have dreamt of traveling to Alpha Centauri to search for an alternative planet to call home, similar to our Earth. Today, my dream is finally becoming a reality.

We have discovered a path leading to Planet 32 in the previous mission, but it has been 7 weeks since we last received an update from the crew. Therefore, our head officer has made the decision to send us on a rescue mission to find the missing team. While this is a rescue mission for them, for me, it presents an opportunity to continue our search for Alpha-Earth.

As I look around my planet today, I see a lot of debris and a harmful environment that wasn't present before. It was once a beautiful blue planet with lush greenery and charming places to call home. My grandparents used to tell me stories about their generation, where people would sit together and share their food and ideas without the need for oxygen gas cylinders hanging on their backs, like we have to use now. We have come to a point where we have trees only in museums and agriculture is now only present in our history books.

If I am fortunate enough to find Alpha-Earth, my first order of business will be to plant a tree and start farming. This was not just my dream, but also that of my brother. He was a part of the second batch of the Alpha-Earth mission, but unfortunately, his crew perished on their journey. They had come across a new creature on Planet 32, but before they could describe it, the creature attacked and killed them. As a result, our captain declared Planet 32 unsuitable for our survival and concluded that Alpha-Earth had yet to be discovered.

In my opinion, it is not acceptable to give up without attempting to overcome the obstacles in our way. My goal is to establish a sustainable relationship with the creatures on Planet 32 and christen it as Alpha-Earth. We must not repeat the same mistakes that our ancestors made on Earth, such as neglecting the pollution levels and the depletion of our natural resources in the name of industrial and economic development.

As our engine starts, we are set to depart in just two minutes. I am hopeful that we will be able to find Alpha-Earth during our journey and establish a positive and sustainable relationship with the species living there.

I apologize for not mentioning this earlier, but the reason behind the changes on our planet was due to a failed biological experiment involving nuclear batteries. Even after a century, we are still struggling to restore our planet to its former glory. Although it may seem like a hypothetical situation, it is hope that motivates us to work towards a better future.

We are currently nearing Planet 32 and closely monitoring the environmental wave and frequency patterns. All indicators suggest that conditions are optimal for our landing. However, we must exercise caution before stepping onto the planet, as we are aware that the creatures inhabiting the planet may not be friendly towards us. As we survey the planet through our droid screen, we can see a creature with three glowing eyes that are brighter than the sun. It appears to be approaching our spaceship, and we must be prepared for any potential danger.

We are currently awaiting orders from our head officer, but unfortunately, the signals appear to be jammed. In spite of this, we are taking a risk and descending onto the planet's surface to confront the dangerous creature. However, upon arrival, we are shocked to see that there are a multitude of creatures surrounding our spaceship, and we may be outnumbered.

Despite the dangerous situation we were facing, it seems that we have stumbled upon a beautiful and lush environment on Planet 32. To our surprise, we see a person with a full beard and leaves covering his body, shouting at our communication camera. Upon zooming in, we realize that it is my brother, who has been living on the planet and surviving with the help of the creatures we had deemed dangerous. He shares with us his incredible journey, describing how the creatures had rescued his crew from a falling spaceship and given them shelter on the planet. Finally, we have found AlphaEarth and achieved a happy ending for all of us.

***

"If you feel you are in a black hole, don't give up. There's a way out."

– Stephen Hawking

BLACK HOLE'S JOURNEY

WRITTEN BY

Yudhvir Singh

REG. NO. - VSFSWC-20220047

CLASS - 7

INDO AMERICAN PUBLIC SCHOOL
UDAIPUR, RAJASTHAN

20

BLACK HOLE'S JOURNEY

"Black holes are not called black because they are black, but because they so rudely steal everything in sight."

– Stephen Hawking

In the year 2530, India had become a developed country. Dr. Cilan, a renowned Indian scientist, was working on a curious project - a spaceship that could safely travel through a black hole and explore its interior. He was relating the spaceship to the concept of space-time, with plans for it to travel at the speed of light - 299,792 km per second, using the formula C = 2.99x10^8 m/s.

One day, while working on the project, a thunderstorm struck. Dr. Cilan stepped out of his lab and saw a blue metal that he had never seen before. He named it 'Dialgamium' and was shocked to discover that it could control time - rewinding and pausing it at will. He quickly fitted the metal into the spaceship and began his journey.

Within seconds, he found himself in front of TON618, the largest known ultra-massive black hole. He bravely piloted the spaceship into the black hole, using his invention to explore its interior.

After five days and six hours, he emerged from the black hole, stunned to realize that he was the only human to have ever survived a journey into a black hole. He felt proud of his invention, but could not transmit any information back to Earth due to the lack of radio waves.

As he looked out of the spaceship, he saw a planet that resembled Earth and decided to land on it. To his shock, he found nothing there except for a recording that said, "Earth is now destroyed. All humans and animals have moved to Planet Onyxide, and Earth has become a devil planet."

Dr. Cilan returned to Earth and shared his discovery with the world, but no one believed him. NASA dismissed it as a mere nightmare, and no one knew whether it was the future of Earth or if Dr. Cilan had ventured into a multiverse, mirror world, or something else entirely.

Despite the skepticism of his peers, Dr. Cilan was determined to uncover the truth about the Earth's fate. He spent years analyzing the data he had collected from the black hole and studying the strange properties of Dialgamium, hoping to find a way to prove his discovery.

Finally, after many long months of intense research, he discovered a way to use Dialgamium to create a portal to the planet Onyxide. He believed that he could use this portal to investigate the claims of the recorder he had found on the Earth-like planet inside the black hole.

With his research complete, Dr. Cilan gathered a team of experts to help him construct the portal. It was a monumental task, but with the help of advanced technology and his own ingenuity, they were able to create a stable gateway to Onyxide.

Dr. Cilan and his team stepped through the portal and found themselves on a planet unlike any they had ever seen before. It was a beautiful world, with lush forests, sparkling oceans, and stunning vistas. But something was off - there were no signs of life anywhere.

As they explored the planet, they began to find clues about what had happened to the people who had been forced to flee there. They discovered ruins of advanced cities, abandoned laboratories, and strange artifacts that hinted at a great catastrophe that had befallen the planet.

As they delved deeper into the mystery, Dr. Cilan realized that he was running out of time. He knew that he had to find a way to return to Earth and warn the people about what he had discovered before it was too late.

With the help of his team, he worked tirelessly to construct a second portal that would allow him to return to Earth. It was a risky endeavor, but he knew that he had to take the chance.

Finally, the day arrived when the portal was complete. Dr. Cilan stepped through it and found himself back on Earth, surrounded by the incredulous stares of his colleagues.

He wasted no time in sharing his findings with the world. He showed them the evidence he had collected and urged them to take action to prevent the same fate from befalling Earth.

Despite the initial skepticism and disbelief, Dr. Cilan's persistence and evidence convinced the world's leaders to take action. They rallied together, using the knowledge and technology that Dr. Cilan had brought back to Earth to prepare for any potential threats.

Years went by, and Earth remained safe from harm. Dr. Cilan became known as a hero, celebrated for his courage and ingenuity in the face of the unknown. His work had saved countless lives and ensured the survival of the human race.

***

“Space exploration is not a choice; it’s an imperative. The more we explore, the more we learn, and the better we can address challenges on Earth.”

– Dr. A. P. J. Abdul Kalam

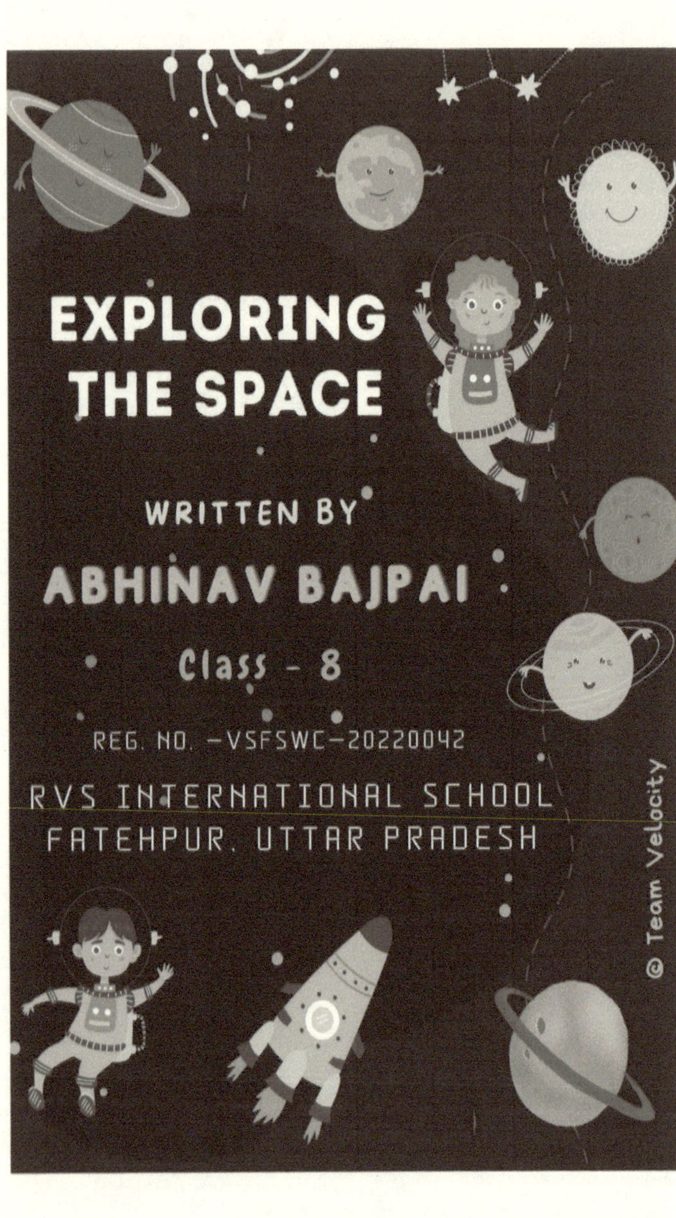
EXPLORING
THE SPACE
WRITTEN BY
ABHINAV BAJPAI
Class - 8
REG. NO. -VSFSWC-20220042
RVS INTERNATIONAL SCHOOL
FATEHPUR, UTTAR PRADESH
© Team Velocity

21

EXPLORING THE SPACE

"This is one small step for a man, one giant leap for mankind."

– Neil Armstrong

Devarsh, Aditi and Raghav had always been fascinated by space and had a lifelong dream of exploring the unknown depths of the cosmos. They were in the 9th grade, and their science teacher had just finished teaching them about our solar system. This had sparked an idea in their minds - what if they could explore space themselves?

Excited about the idea, Devarsh, Aditi, and Raghav started brainstorming ways to turn their dream into a reality. They spent countless hours researching space exploration, studying the achievements of astronauts, and delving into the mysteries of the universe. Their passion and determination fueled their pursuit.

One day, while browsing the internet for space-related news, they stumbled upon a remarkable discovery. A space agency called StellarX was offering a unique opportunity for young aspiring space explorers. StellarX had launched a program called "Stars of Tomorrow," aimed at providing students with the chance to embark on a space exploration mission.

Overjoyed by this incredible opportunity, Devarsh, Aditi, and Raghav decided to apply immediately. They eagerly filled out the application forms, detailing their passion for space, their scientific knowledge, and their unwavering dedication to the pursuit of knowledge beyond Earth's boundaries.

Weeks passed, and the friends grew increasingly anxious, eagerly awaiting news of their application status. Finally, one fateful evening, they received an email from StellarX. Their hearts raced as they read the message, and to their delight, they were accepted into the program. Their dream was about to become a reality.

The friends couldn't contain their excitement as they made preparations for the upcoming space exploration mission. They underwent rigorous physical and mental training, learning about the challenges they would face in the harsh environment of space. They familiarized themselves with the spacecraft, its controls, and safety protocols. The spacecraft was equipped with state-of-the-art technology, including advanced navigation systems and high-tech telescopes.

The day of the mission arrived, and the three friends, dressed in their sleek spacesuits, stood before the grand spaceship that would carry them to the space to each of the planets in our solar system.. A crowd had gathered to witness the historic moment. The friends waved to their families, who were brimming with pride and support, and then stepped onto the spacecraft.

As the engines roared to life, Devarsh, Aditi, and Raghav felt a mixture of exhilaration and nervousness.

The countdown commenced, and with each passing second, their dreams drew closer to reality. At zero, the spaceship soared into the sky, leaving Earth's atmosphere behind. The three friends were beyond excited to embark on this once-in-a-lifetime journey.

Days turned into weeks as their spacecraft traversed the vast expanse of space, each passing moment bringing them closer to their first destination: the Moon. The friends marveled at the beauty of Earth from space, watching its blue-green hues fade into the darkness of the cosmos. Upon reaching the Moon, they embarked on lunar excursions, exploring its desolate yet enchanting landscape. They collected rock samples, conducted experiments, and absorbed the serenity of Earth's celestial companion. The Moon became their training ground, a stepping stone towards their ultimate goal.

Their next destination was Mercury, the closest planet to the Sun. The spacecraft gracefully glided through space, and after a few hours, they arrived at their destination. As they approached Mercury, they marvelled at its barren and rocky landscape. The intense heat made it impossible to land, but they had the chance to observe its cratered surface from the safety of their spacecraft.

Next on their itinerary was Venus, known as Earth's twin due to its similar size and composition. However, they quickly realized that Venus was a hostile environment. Thick clouds of sulphuric acid and poisonous gases blanketed the planet, creating a greenhouse effect that made it hotter than any other planet in the solar system. They admired Venus's beauty from a safe distance, capturing breath-taking images and scientific data to share with their school and moved on to Earth's neighbour, Mars.

Mars was the first planet where they were able to land. They marvelled at the rusty landscape and explored the valleys, canyons, and ancient riverbeds. They explored its red deserts and even found evidence of water on the planet. It was on Mars that they discovered intriguing rock formations that hinted at the possibility of past water flows. The significance of their find filled them with a sense of accomplishment and wonder.

They continued their journey to the gas giants of the outer solar system - Jupiter, Saturn, Uranus, and Neptune. These planets were massive and had incredible ring systems. The friends were astounded by the sheer magnitude of these colossal planets and their magnificent ring systems. The swirling clouds and vibrant hues painted an otherworldly picture, leaving them in awe of nature's artistry.

However, the journey was not without its challenges. The spacecraft had to navigate through the treacherous asteroid belt, a region teeming with rocky debris. They faced a significant challenge while crossing the asteroid belt. The friends experienced heart-stopping moments as they dodged and weaved through the labyrinth of asteroids. They felt a profound sense of relief when they emerged safely on the other side, their spacecraft slightly battered but intact. The spacecraft was hit by several small asteroids, but fortunately, they were able to fix the damage and continue their journey.

Finally, they reached the biggest planet in our solar system, Jupiter. It was a gaseous planet with a raging storm known as the Great Red Spot. Its immense size and powerful magnetic field were unlike anything they had encountered before. They were amazed by its size and the unique features of its many moons. The Great Red Spot, a gigantic storm that had raged for centuries, captivated their attention. The friends observed the tempest from a safe distance, documenting its swirling motions and capturing its magnificence through the spacecraft's cameras.

As they prepared to land on Jupiter, they encountered a new problem - the lack of a solid surface. They had to navigate through the thick atmosphere, and the pressure and temperature were incredibly high. However, with the help of their spacecraft, they were able to land on a small patch of solid ground on one of Jupiter's moons.

The moon they landed on was Io, known for its volcanic activity. They marveled at the sight of towering volcanoes and bubbling lava lakes. The landscape was unlike anything they had ever seen before.

While exploring Io, they made a remarkable discovery. They found evidence of microbial life in the sulfur-rich volcanic soil. It was a groundbreaking revelation, indicating the possibility of life existing in extreme environments.

Excited by their discovery, they collected samples and documented their findings. They knew that their discovery would reshape our understanding of the potential for life beyond Earth.

After spending a few days exploring Io, they bid farewell to the volcanic moon and set their sights on their next destination, Saturn. The journey through space was awe-inspiring, with stunning views of Saturn's rings and its many moons.

Upon reaching Saturn, they were captivated by the planet's mesmerizing beauty. The rings, made up of icy particles, encircled the gas giant in a magnificent display. They carefully maneuvered their spacecraft through the intricate gaps in the rings, witnessing their ethereal grandeur up close.

They also had the opportunity to visit Saturn's largest moon, Titan. Its dense atmosphere and hydrocarbon lakes fascinated them. They conducted experiments and collected data, expanding our knowledge of this unique celestial body.

Their journey continued to the outer planets, Uranus and Neptune. These distant giants, shrouded in mystery, revealed breathtaking sights. Uranus, with its unique tilted axis, offered stunning views of its icy blue atmosphere. Neptune, with its vivid blue color and swirling storms, left them in awe of its majestic nature.

As they ventured deeper into space, they encountered celestial wonders beyond their wildest imagination. They witnessed the birth of stars in massive nebulas, observed distant galaxies, and marveled at the cosmic ballet of celestial bodies.

Their journey through the cosmos had transformed them. They had not only fulfilled their lifelong dream of exploring space but had also contributed to scientific knowledge and made groundbreaking discoveries.

With their mission nearing its end, they embarked on the long journey back to Earth, carrying a treasure trove of data, samples, and memories. They couldn't wait to share their experiences and findings with the scientific community and inspire future generations of explorers.

As they re-entered Earth's atmosphere, a profound sense of gratitude and accomplishment washed over them. They had come a long way from their 9th-grade classroom, fueled by curiosity and passion. They had followed their dreams, defied the boundaries of what seemed possible, and ventured into the unknown depths of the cosmos.

Devarsh, Aditi and Raghav's journey was not just a story of exploration but a testament to the indomitable spirit of humanity. Their quest to unravel the mysteries of the universe had ignited a spark in the hearts of countless others, inspiring a new generation of explorers to reach for the stars and embrace the wonders of the cosmos.

***

A Day
in
Euthopia
WRITTEN BY
Aadarsh Deepak Meshram
Reg. No.- VSFSWC-20220003
CLASS – 7
SPACE CENTRAL SCHOOL, SRIHARIKOTA
NELLORE, ANDHRA PRADESH
© Team Velocity

22

A DAY IN EUTHOPIA

"I suppose the one quality in an astronaut more powerful than any other is curiosity. They have to get some place nobody's ever been."

– John Glenn

It was a lazy Sunday morning, and Sachin, a seventh-grade student, was still snuggled up in bed. He had been up late the previous night, working on a school project. He had to create a model of the solar system and explain the planetary movements. He had been engrossed in his work, fascinated by the intricacies of the universe and the planets that made it up.

The sound of his mother's voice calling his name and the aroma of freshly cooked breakfast wafted into his room, but he was in no hurry to get up. His mother's voice grew louder as she urged him to wake up and come to the breakfast table where his father and sister were waiting.

Finally, Sachin dragged himself out of bed, rubbing the sleep from his eyes. He made his way to the kitchen, and his nose immediately perked up at the scent of his favorite breakfast - Aaloo Paratha with curd and pickle. His mother had outdone herself this time.

The kitchen was brightly lit, and the sun streamed in through the window, casting a warm glow over the room. Sachin's sister, Mayra, who was a high school student, was already seated at the table, chatting with his father, while waiting for her little brother. They welcomed Sachin with smiles and talked about how excited they were to spend the day together.

Sachin sat down at the table, and his mother served him a piping hot paratha. He took a bite and savored the crispy exterior and the soft, warm filling of mashed potatoes. The tangy curd and the spicy pickle were the perfect accompaniments, and Sachin felt his taste buds dance with joy.

He had always loved potatoes, not just because of their taste but also because they reminded him of the universe. Whenever he saw a basket full of potatoes, he imagined that all the planets and asteroids had gathered for a meeting, which would be led by the Sun. As he ate, Sachin's mind wandered to his science lessons. He loved learning about the vastness of space, the mysteries of the cosmos, and the planets and stars that made up the universe.

As Sachin continued to eat his breakfast, he couldn't help but ponder over the vastness of the universe. He turned to his father and asked, "Dad, how was the universe created? I mean, how did it all start?"

His father smiled and replied, "Well, there are different theories about the origin of the universe, but the most widely accepted one is the Big Bang theory. It suggests that the universe was born around 13.8 billion years ago from a single point, which was extremely hot and dense. Then, there was a sudden explosion, and the universe started to expand rapidly."

Mayra, who was equally curious, added, "But how was the planet Earth formed? Was it there from the beginning?"

Their father replied, "No, the Earth was not there from the beginning. It formed around 4.5 billion years ago from the dust and gas that surrounded the young sun. Over time, this dust and gas came together due to gravity, forming the planets, including Earth."

Sachin's eyes widened with amazement, and he asked, "So, what makes Earth so special that it can sustain life? I mean, why is it not too hot or too cold?"

Their father explained, "The Earth is at the right distance from the Sun, neither too close nor too far, which makes it the perfect place for life to thrive. It also has an atmosphere that protects us from harmful radiation and a magnetic field that shields us from solar winds."

Mayra, who was always fascinated by astronomy, asked, "Dad, do you think there could be life on other planets?"

Their father replied, "It's definitely possible. We have already discovered many exoplanets that have conditions similar to Earth, and scientists are continuously searching for signs of life beyond our planet."

Seeing the curiosity in Sachin and Mayra's eyes, their father decided to make a plan to take them to a space planetarium. He suggested, "Hey, why don't we go to the planetarium today? You can see the wonders of the universe and learn more about it."

Sachin and Mayra's faces lit up with excitement, and they both nodded eagerly.

After finishing their delicious breakfast, Sachin and his sister Mayra were bursting with excitement to go to the planetarium. They quickly got ready, changing their clothes, and grabbing their backpacks filled with snacks and water bottles.

Their father, who had already planned the outing, was waiting for them outside, and they all got into the car and drove to the planetarium.

ઌ

As they reached the planetarium, they were amazed by the size of the planetarium, a giant dome-shaped structure with a metallic sheen reflecting the sun's rays and the various exhibits on display. Sachin and Mayra couldn't wait to explore and learn more about the universe.

Their father guided them through the exhibits, pointing out the different planets, stars, and galaxies. Sachin and Mayra were fascinated by the models of the solar system and the interactive displays that allowed them to learn about the formation of planets and stars.

As they walked through the exhibits, they learned about the history of space exploration and the various missions that had been sent to study the universe. They were amazed by the images captured by the Hubble Space Telescope and the beautiful colors and patterns of the nebulae and galaxies.

Inside the planetarium, they found themselves in a vast and dark hall. The only source of light came from the enormous dome-shaped screen in front of them. As they settled into their seats, the lights went off, and the screen lit up with stars and galaxies, taking them on a breathtaking virtual tour of the universe.

As they watched the virtual tour of the universe, Sachin and Mayra were completely mesmerized. They saw stars, galaxies, and nebulas that they had never seen before.

Suddenly, they were pulled towards the center of the universe by some source of light. They could feel themselves floating in space, and they couldn't believe what was happening. As they looked around, they realized that it was completely dark, and they couldn't see anything around them except for each other. They were both scared and unsure of what was happening to them. As they floated in the darkness, they couldn't help but wonder if they were really in space or if it was all just a part of the virtual tour.

As Sachin and Mayra looked around, they realized that they were no longer floating in space. They had landed on a planet that looked like Earth, with an atmosphere full of water and oxygen. At first, they thought they had somehow returned home, but their excitement quickly turned to fear as they saw some strange creatures approaching them.

These creatures had four eyes, two on the back of their heads and two on the front. They also had two small noses, one on the front and one on the back, and two long ears. Despite their small stature, they didn't have any hair on their heads, and they seemed to be looking directly at Sachin and Mayra.

Sachin and Mayra were trembling with fear. They had never seen such creatures before, and they stood still in shock, not knowing what to do next. Suddenly, strange creatures approached them, and to their surprise, they started speaking in a language that they could understand. The creatures could see the fear in the children's eyes, and one of them said, "Don't be afraid, we won't harm you."

Sachin and Mayra were still unsure of what was happening, but they realized that they had somehow landed on an unknown planet. The creatures noticed the confusion on their faces and introduced himself as Tomu.

Tomu explained to them that they are on the planet Euthopia in the whirlpool galaxy, which was similar to Earth but had a few differences in weather and atmospheric conditions. Tomu also explained that the creatures on this planet had evolved differently, resulting in unique physical characteristics. The siblings listened intently, trying to make sense of what was happening around them.

Sachin and Mayra looked at each other, surprised by Tomu's revelation. They couldn't believe that they were on a different planet altogether.

Mayra asked Tomu, "What is meant by Euthoia"?

Tomu replied, "Euthopia is a society where people have superhuman abilities. They can fly, read minds, or manipulate matter with their thoughts. People spend their day using their abilities to help others, or pursuing their passions and hobbies."

Suddenly, Sachin spoke up, "How do you know that we are from planet Earth?"

Tomu smiled and replied, "We have been monitoring the galaxy for quite long time, and we have picked up signals from your planet. We have been eagerly waiting for visitors from Earth."

Sachin and Mayra were amazed by Tomu's response, and they looked around in wonder, trying to take in the magnitude of the situation.

Tomu continued to explain to Sachin and Mayra about the history of his planet. "Euthopia was born long before your planet Earth. Our planet has existed for billions of years, and it has undergone many transformations over time."

Tomu's words piqued Sachin and Mayra's interest even further. "Wow, that's amazing! What kind of advanced technology do you have that allows you to see all other galaxies?" asked Mayra.

Tomu smiled and explained, "We have developed highly sophisticated telescopes that allow us to observe galaxies and celestial bodies from afar. Our telescopes use advanced imaging techniques and powerful algorithms to map the cosmos and reveal its mysteries."

After explaining their technology, Tomu took Sachin and Mayra to his laboratory where he showed them some of the advanced technologies that his planet had developed. The siblings were amazed to see the futuristic machines and gadgets that they had never seen before.

As they walked through the laboratory, Tomu stopped in front of a large screen that displayed the view of the planet Earth from Euthopia. Sachin and Mayra were surprised to see their own planet from such a far distance.

Tomu smiled and said, “Would you like to see your planet up close?”

Sachin and Mayra nodded their heads enthusiastically.

Tomu took them to a small room where they sat down in front of a large screen. Tomu worked on a few buttons and suddenly the screen showed a live feed of planet Earth from the perspective of Euthopia.

Sachin and Mayra couldn’t believe their eyes as they saw the beauty of their planet from a completely different angle. They saw the vast oceans, the lush green forests, the towering mountains, and the sprawling cities, all from a completely different viewpoint.

Tomu then showed them some of the advanced technologies that his planet had developed, including teleportation and anti-gravity machines. Sachin and Mayra were amazed at the level of advancement that the planet Euthopia had achieved.

As their visit came to an end, Tomu said, “I hope you had a wonderful time on our planet. We welcome you to visit us again, anytime you want.”

Suddenly, the lights of the dark hall switched on, and Sachin and Mayra found themselves back in the planetarium. They looked at each other, surprised by the sudden change of scenery.

As they made their way out of the planetarium, Sachin and Mayra couldn’t stop talking about their amazing adventure. They couldn’t believe that they had traveled to a different planet and met creatures from another world. They were grateful to their father for taking them on such an incredible trip and for igniting their curiosity about the universe.

As they drove back home, Sachin and Mayra couldn't wait to go back to school and share their newfound knowledge with their classmates. They were already making plans to come back to the planetarium and learn even more about the mysteries of the cosmos. They were filled with excitement and wonder, knowing that there was so much more to the universe than they had ever imagined.

From that day forward, Sachin and Mayra were even more interested in astronomy and space exploration. They spent many nights stargazing and dreaming of their next adventure in the universe. And they knew that one day, they would go back to Euthopia and explore the mysteries of the cosmos with their new friend Tomu.

THE DOWN RANGE

WRITTEN BY

HASINI REDDY

REG. NO. - VSFSWC-20220047

CLASS-9

PADMAVATHI VIDYALAYA

NELLORE, ANDHRA PRADESH

23

THE DOWN RANGE

"Space travel for everyone is the next frontier in the human experience"

– Buzz Aldrin

Once upon a time, there were two friends, Aditya and Roshan, who were passionate scientists. They were not just dreamers; they had a passion for exploration and innovation. Their big dream was to make space accessible to everyone. Together, they worked tirelessly to turn their dream into reality. They started sending humans to space through their space tourism company. They built a space station in orbit called "Down Range," from which they controlled all the operations of their space tourism venture.

Aditya specialized in astrophysics and space engineering. His expertise lay in understanding the vastness of the universe, the behavior of celestial bodies, and the intricacies of space travel. With his deep knowledge and analytical skills, he was able to design and construct spaceships that could safely transport tourists into the great unknown. Aditya's attention to detail and commitment to safety made him a trusted figure in the space industry.

On the other hand, Roshan was a masterful engineer and inventor. His creativity knew no bounds, and he excelled in designing cutting-edge technology that complemented Aditya's ambitious projects. Roshan's expertise spanned robotics, artificial intelligence, and spacecraft systems. His inventions played a crucial role in making space tourism not just safe but also comfortable and immersive for the tourists. Roshan's inventions, including the remarkable lady robot Hasini, revolutionized the way humans interacted with the cosmos.

Inside the Down Range space station, a fantastic display showcased the trajectory of all the spaceships and provided live updates on their status. In the spacecraft control room, the lady robot named Hasini diligently monitored all the events, ensuring that everything remained in order. Hasini played a crucial role in keeping Aditya and Roshan informed of real-time information. Her constant updates allowed them to oversee operations with confidence, ensuring that everything ran smoothly and safely.

Hasini was an integral part of Aditya and Roshan's space tourism venture. With her advanced capabilities in robotics and artificial intelligence, Hasini brought a new level of efficiency and assistance to the operations of the Down Range space station. Her vast database of information and her ability to process complex data made her an invaluable resource. Hasini's primary responsibility was to monitor all the events within the space station and ensure that everything was running smoothly. Her keen sensors and analytical algorithms allowed her to detect any potential issues or anomalies, providing early warnings to Aditya and Roshan. With Hasini's constant vigilance, they could promptly address any concerns and maintain a safe environment for the crew and tourists.

Moreover, Hasini's interactions with the tourists brought an element of comfort and familiarity to their space journey. Her warm personality, combined with her extensive knowledge of space and the cosmos, made her an excellent companion during the tourists' exploration. Whether explaining the wonders of the universe or engaging in casual conversations, Hasini enhanced the overall experience and made the journey even more memorable.

Hasini's presence in the Down Range space station truly revolutionized the way humans interacted with technology and space. She exemplified the potential of artificial intelligence and robotics, showing that these advancements could be both practical and compassionate. Through her assistance and companionship, Hasini became an essential member of the team, supporting Aditya and Roshan's vision to make space accessible to everyone.

One day, something unexpected happened. An alien, from faraway Uranus, decided to hijack one of the spaceships that was visiting the Moon. The alien wanted to take control of the advanced technology on board for its own purposes. It was a scary situation for Aditya, Roshan, and especially for the tourists on the spaceship.

As soon as Hasini noticed the trouble, she sprang into action. She immediately went into action mode, analyzing the situation and making a plan to rescue the tourists. With her quick thinking and advanced knowledge, she knew she had to go to Uranus to confront the alien and bring everyone back safely.

Hasini bravely journeyed to Uranus, a planet unlike any she had seen before. When she arrived, she faced the alien, who was much bigger and stronger. But Hasini was determined to protect the lives of the tourists and save the day. She used her combat skills and clever strategies to outmaneuver the alien, dodging its attacks while landing her own blows.

The battle between Hasini and the alien was intense and filled with suspense. Hasini fought with all her might, never giving up. She knew that the tourists were counting on her to bring them back home safely.

Finally, after a fierce struggle, Hasini succeeded in defeating the alien and rescued the spaceship and all the tourists. Everyone was overjoyed and immensely grateful to Hasini for her bravery and heroism. Aditya and Roshan were incredibly proud of their friend and the remarkable lady robot they had created.

Word of Hasini's courageous act spread throughout the galaxy, and she became an inspiration to others. Her story reminded everyone that no matter how big the challenge, with determination and courage, one can overcome any obstacle.

From that day forward, Aditya, Roshan, and Hasini continued their space tourism ventures with renewed confidence. They knew that together they could face any adventure that awaited them among the stars. And as they explored the wonders of the universe, they were grateful for the friendships they had formed and the incredible experiences that lay ahead. With Down Range as their Launchpad, they soared to new heights, inspiring generations to reach for the stars.

WRITTEN BY

Shashwat Bajpai

Class - 8

REG. NO. -VSFSWC-20220177

RVS INTERNATIONAL SCHOOL
FATEHPUR, UTTAR PRADESH

24

THE RED PLANET

"The solar system is completely wide open. Almost anywhere we go, I'm sure we would learn a lot."

– Alan Stern

There was a rush of people heading to Florida to witness the first-ever launch of the "Mission Mars" spacecraft. The air was filled with excitement and anticipation, except for 10 families who were anxious about their loved ones who were venturing into space for the first time. Among these families was Jack Carlson, who was overcome with excitement as it had been his lifelong dream to explore Mars.

Jack Carlson had always been fascinated by space exploration. From a young age, he had dreamed of venturing beyond Earth and setting foot on the red planet, Mars. Now, as he stood among the crowd and crew members gathered in Florida to witness the launch of the Mission Mars spacecraft, his heart raced with a mix of excitement and nervousness.

As the countdown began, Jack's heart pounded in his chest. All the crew members entered into the spaceship. The immense rocket towered above him, ready to propel him and the rest of the crew into the unknown. The excitement in the air was palpable, mingled with a sense of history being made.

"Ten...nine...eight..." The crowd's voices grew louder as the countdown progressed. Jack's pulse quickened and he exchanged excited glances with his fellow crew members. They had trained for years for this moment, and now they were on the cusp of fulfilling their shared dream.

"Three...two...one...ignition!"

With a deafening roar, the engines ignited, and the spacecraft lifted off the Launchpad. Jack felt the tremendous force pressing him into his seat as the rocket pierced through the atmosphere. The Earth slowly shrank below, its blue hues blending with the vastness of space.

Inside the spacecraft, the crew experienced a mix of awe and disbelief. Weightlessness enveloped them, and they floated gracefully, their excitement building with each passing moment. As they coasted towards Mars, Jack couldn't help but gaze out of the window, marveling at the shimmering stars that adorned the black canvas of space.

Days turned into weeks as the crew journeyed through the vastness of space. They meticulously carried out their mission tasks, conducting experiments, monitoring systems, and preparing for their arrival on Mars. The crew's camaraderie and support for one another buoyed their spirits, even during moments of homesickness.

Finally, after a long and arduous journey, the spacecraft entered the Martian atmosphere. The tension on board grew palpable as the crew prepared for the crucial landing. Jack's heart raced as he watched the planet's surface approach rapidly.

However, as the spacecraft was about to land on the Mars, its controls failed and communication with Earth was lost. The spacecraft crashed onto the surface of Mars, causing six crew members to collapse, leaving only four crew members conscious. Jack Carlson, Emily Jackson, Peter, and Allen were among the survivors, but Peter and Allen were badly injured.

After a few hours, they regained consciousness and found themselves stranded on the barren, red planet. The conscious crew members quickly regained their composure and activated the emergency protocols they had trained for. They looked around and saw nothing but red mountains and reddish soil. As the gravity on Mars is less than that of Earth, they felt their weight reduced. They radioed for assistance, desperately trying to establish communication with Earth. Fear and worry gripped their hearts, but they knew they had to remain focused and determined.

Hours turned into days as the crew worked tirelessly to stabilize their situation. With limited resources and no immediate help from Earth, they relied on their skills and ingenuity to survive. They refused to give in to despair, determined to overcome the challenges they faced.

They decided to explore Mars and gathered all the necessary items from the spacecraft before setting out. During this time, they made remarkable discoveries and contributions to the understanding of the

Martian environment. They conducted experiments, collected samples, and documented their experiences. Unfortunately, after 16 days, Peter passed away due to an infection in his wound, and Allen's health was also deteriorating. A few days later, they lost Allen as well.

The loss of their fellow crew members, Peter and Allen, was a devastating blow to Jack and Emily. Grief weighed heavily on their hearts as they mourned the loss of their friends and companions. Yet, their determination to explore Mars and honor their fallen comrades pushed them forward. Jack and Emily continued their journey across the Martian landscape, driven by a sense of purpose and the need to make their mission count.

Days turned into weeks, and Jack and Emily experienced both the wonders and challenges of life on Mars. They faced extreme temperature fluctuations, limited resources, and the constant need for vigilance. But their resilience and shared sense of purpose fueled their determination to continue their mission.

Their communication with Earth remained sporadic, but they kept sending updates and data, hoping that their discoveries would inspire future missions and scientific breakthroughs. They pressed on, aware that every step they took on the red planet contributed to humanity's understanding of the universe.

After weeks of traversing the Martian landscape, Jack and Emily were startled to come across a small boy. He appeared to be around 10 years old, with dusty clothes and a worn-out backpack slung over his shoulder. They couldn't believe their eyes. A human child on Mars?

Filled with curiosity and concern, they approached the boy cautiously. Jack knelt down to the boy's eye level and gently asked, "How did you get here? Are you lost?"

The boy looked up at them with wide, innocent eyes and replied, "I came from Earth through a tunnel."

Jack and Emily exchanged puzzled glances. The possibility of a tunnel connecting Earth and Mars seemed unfathomable, but they couldn't ignore the boy's words. Intrigued, they pressed further, "Can you tell us more about this tunnel? Where is it?"

The boy hesitated for a moment before sharing, "I found a hidden cave, and inside there was a strange machine. When I touched it, a portal opened up, and I ended up here on Mars."

Jack and Emily couldn't help but be both skeptical and intrigued by the boy's story. If such a tunnel did exist, it could revolutionize space travel and open up new possibilities for human colonization on Mars. Determined to investigate further, they asked the boy to lead them back to the hidden cave.

Guided by the boy, they journeyed through the rugged Martian terrain until they arrived at a secluded cave entrance. As they cautiously entered, their eyes widened in disbelief. Inside the cave, they discovered an intricately designed device unlike anything they had ever seen before.

It resembled a complex teleportation device, with enigmatic symbols etched on its surface. It emitted a faint hum, indicating that it was still operational. Jack and Emily exchanged amazed glances, realizing the immense potential this discovery held.

Filled with a mix of excitement and trepidation, they contemplated whether to test the device themselves. They knew it was a risky proposition, but the lure of unraveling the mysteries of the tunnel and potentially returning to Earth was too tempting to resist.

After careful deliberation, Jack made up his mind. He turned to Emily and said, "We've come this far, and if there's a chance that this device can take us back to Earth, we have to try. We owe it to ourselves and to all those who dream of exploring the stars."

Emily nodded in agreement, understanding the weight of their decision. With cautious anticipation, they activated the device, its energy pulsating and enveloping them in a mesmerizing glow. In an instant, they were engulfed by a surge of energy, and their surroundings transformed.

When the light subsided, Jack and Emily found themselves standing in a familiar place. They were back on Earth. Overwhelmed by a rush of emotions, they gazed at the blue sky above, breathing in the familiar scent of the Earth's air. They had made an astonishing journey from Mars to Earth through an extraordinary tunnel.

News of their return spread quickly, captivating the world's attention. Scientists, governments, and space agencies clamored to study the teleportation device and unravel its secrets. Jack and Emily became overnight celebrities, hailed as pioneers of interplanetary travel.

As research and experimentation progressed, the technology behind the tunnel was gradually understood. It turned out to be a marvel of advanced extraterrestrial engineering, surpassing any human-made technology. The device provided humanity with a newfound understanding of space-time manipulation and paved the way for further exploration of the cosmos.

Jack and Emily continued to play a pivotal role in unlocking the secrets of the teleportation device. They became respected figures in the scientific community, advocating for responsible exploration and harnessing the newfound knowledge to benefit humanity.

Their journey from Mars to Earth through the tunnel became a symbol of human resilience, curiosity, and the unyielding spirit of exploration. It marked a turning point in history, propelling humanity to new frontiers and igniting a global fascination with the mysteries of the universe.

Jack and Emily's legacy extended far beyond their own extraordinary experience. Their determination and thirst for knowledge inspired countless individuals to push the boundaries of what was considered possible. The boy they encountered on Mars became a symbol of hope, reminding humanity that even in the most unlikely of circumstances, extraordinary discoveries can be made.

Together, they embarked on a new chapter of human exploration, driven by the belief that the universe held endless wonders waiting to be uncovered.

***

The Golden Man
Written By
Ayman Nadeem Khan
Class - 5
Indian School Al-Ghubra
Muscat, Oman
REG. NO. - VSFSWC-20220144
@ Team Velocity

25

THE GOLDEN MAN

"The mystery of human existence lies not in just staying alive, but in finding something to live for."

– Fyodor Dostoevsky

Once upon a time, in the year 1613, there was a daring man named Andrew Holland. He was a tall man, with broad shoulders and a muscular build. He had piercing blue eyes and a strong jawline. His hair was a wild mess of curls that often fell in front of his face. He had a quick wit and was known for his sharp tongue, which often got him into trouble.

Despite his rough exterior, Andrew had a kind heart and was always willing to help those in need. He had a reputation for being fearless and would often take on challenges that others would shy away from. Andrew was an adventurous soul who loved to explore the unknown and was always seeking new experiences.

Despite his adventurous spirit and intelligence, Andrew had a flaw - he was a lazy person who was not willing to do any job. This made his family frustrated with him as they struggled to make ends meet. Andrew's parents and siblings had to work hard to provide for the family while he lazed around all day. They repeatedly urged him to get a job, but Andrew was not interested.

He preferred to spend his days dreaming about his next adventure, rather than working to support himself and his family. This behavior caused tensions within the family, and Andrew's parents worried about his future.

Andrew lived happily with his family until tragedy struck in 1614 when they were involved in a devastating accident. Unfortunately, Andrew's family did not survive the accident, and Andrew himself sustained severe injuries.

The accident left Andrew devastated and alone. He had lost the only people who mattered to him, and he had no idea what to do next. He found it hard to move on from the loss, and his injuries only made things worse. Andrew struggled to perform even the simplest of tasks, and he became even more lazy and unmotivated than he was before. He would spend most of his days lying in bed, lost in his thoughts and feeling sorry for himself. The only thing that seemed to give him any comfort was his love for books. He would read for hours on end, lost in the pages of adventure stories and tales of bravery.

It took a year, until 1615, for him to be completely recovered from the injuries. During his time in the hospital, Andrew had a lot of time to reflect on his life and the direction it had taken. He felt a deep sense of regret for not having done more with his life before the accident. He realized that he had been wasting his potential and had not been living up to his own expectations or the expectations of his family. As a result, Andrew became determined to turn his life around and make something of him.

One day he went in search of a job, but despite his best efforts, he was unable to secure employment. Feeling dejected, he decided to venture into the jungle and live there.

Andrew spent several weeks in the jungle, struggling to survive. He built himself a small hut made of branches and leaves to protect himself from the elements. Nearby, he found a stream that provided him with fresh water, and he learned how to catch fish and gather fruits and vegetables from the surrounding forest. Despite the challenges he faced, Andrew found a sense of peace and solitude in the jungle that he had never experienced before.

One day, feeling tired of only eating and sleeping, Andrew set out to explore the forest. As he roamed through the dense forest, Andrew stumbled upon a mysterious cave. It was unlike anything he had ever seen before, and he felt drawn to explore its depths.

As he made his way through the cave, he discovered a hidden chamber filled with ancient artifacts and treasures, including gold, diamonds, and iron. To his amazement, he also found a treasure box belonging to an ancient Egyptian king, which contained a vast amount of diamonds.

Excited by his discovery, Andrew decided to fashion a suit of armor using the gold he had found in the cave, along with a few of the diamonds he had discovered. However, he had to be careful, as the cave was also home to molten lava. He melted the gold and shaped it into a suit, which he left outside the cave to cool.

As he waited for the gold to cool down, Andrew explored the surrounding area and stumbled upon a river. He noticed that the river had some peculiar rocks that looked like they had been carved. He picked up one of the rocks and examined it closely, and to his surprise, he discovered that it was a rare gemstone that glowed in the dark. He collected a few of these stones and decided to use them to decorate his suit of armor.

Once the gold had cooled, Andrew put on his new armor and marveled at how it glimmered in the sunlight. He felt like a new man and decided to name himself the "The Golden Man,". With his new armor and weapons, he felt invincible and ready to take on the world as a hero.

After enjoying his moment as "The Golden Man," Andrew eventually removed the suit of armor and gathered all the diamonds he had found in the cave. With the profits from selling the diamonds, he was able to amass an incredible fortune of $516.2 billion. With this newfound wealth, he bought a large house and set up a laboratory where he could experiment and improve upon his armor.

Eager to enhance the capabilities of his armor, Andrew developed the technology that could help his suit fly and shoot. After acquiring the necessary items, he added them to his suit and was thrilled to discover that he could now take flight while wearing it.

Andrew, now "The Golden Man," decided to use his newfound strength and abilities to help those in need. He roamed the countryside, searching for any trouble he could find. He used his strength to rescue people from burning buildings, fight off bandits, and protect the innocent.

The people he helped soon started to spread tales of his heroic deeds, and word of "The Golden Man" spread far and wide. People started to look up to him as a symbol of hope, and Andrew was finally able to find the purpose he had been searching for.

Despite his newfound fame, Andrew remained humble and continued to help those in need. He knew that the real reward was in the gratitude of the people he had helped, and he felt fulfilled knowing that he was making a difference in the world.

Suddenly, a group of evil aliens appeared with their nefarious plan to destroy the earth and rule over it. Without warning, they launched an atomic bomb that destroyed entire cities in Belgium, Bangladesh, Russia, and China. The world was in chaos and people were scared for their lives. Andrew knew that he had to act quickly to prevent the aliens from causing any further destruction.

Determined to save the world, Andrew put on his golden armor and set out to fight the aliens. He had never fought anything like this before, but he was not afraid. He flew into the air, chasing the alien's spaceships and firing his laser beam at them. The aliens tried to fight back with their advanced technology, but Andrew's armor was too strong for their weapons.

As he battled the aliens, Andrew noticed a weakness in their shields. He exploited this and flew into the alien's spaceship, where he confronted their leader. The alien leader was a massive creature with tentacles, who towered over Andrew. However, Andrew was not intimidated. He charged towards the alien leader, his golden armor glistening in the dimly lit spaceship.

In a fierce battle, Andrew used all his strength and knowledge of combat to defeat the alien leader. With the leader's defeat, the other aliens surrendered and retreated back to their planet. Andrew had saved the world from certain doom.

Andrew's heroic actions quickly made him a worldwide sensation. The people of the world cheered and thanked Andrew for his bravery. He had become a hero, and his name would be remembered for generations to come. Andrew knew that his adventure wasn't over yet, and that he would continue to use his golden armor to protect the world from any threats that might come in the future.

Inspired by his bravery, he formed his own team of superheroes called "The Peacerals" to help protect the earth from future threats. Together, they worked to maintain peace and harmony throughout the world, and their efforts helped to ensure that humanity could thrive in safety and security.

***

INVITED STORIES

THE GREAT LEGEND OF AARADHY
WRITTEN BY
AARADHY SHARMA
CLASS - 4
DELHI PUBLIC SCHOOL, BOPAL
AHMEDABAD, GUJARAT
© Team Velocity

26

THE GREAT LEGEND OF AARADHY

"The things that make us different, those are our superpowers"

– Lena Waithe

So… it's the year 2030, and a person named Aaradhy has developed technology that gives him the power of a god. However, not everyone has access to this technology, only Aaradhy has it. He also has an intelligent brother named Atharv. Both of them are very smart. You might think that this technology has made the world peaceful, but unfortunately, that's not the case. There is a devil named AST-5O4, and Aaradhy and Atharv, also known as the "A/A GANG," are fighting to defend the world against him. AST-5O4 has never been able to defeat Aaradhy and Atharv.

The devil also says, 'I'll have my revenge soon,' but he always loses.

Now, let's get into the actual story.

One day, the A/As were informed through their calculator that AST-5O4 was nearby.

"What, a new mission already?" said Atharv.

"Well, we gotta go with it," replied Aaradhy.

“Man, I’m so sick of this,” Atharv said in an irritated tone.

“I guess we gotta rush,” said Aaradhy.

“Yeah,” replied Atharv.

They ran and quickly arrived at the location.

Then AST-5O4 taunted them again, “I’m more powerful than ever, even more powerful than you and your little brother!”

Aaradhy replied, “Well, let’s see about that!” and Using his powers, he tried to stop the monster, moving at a speed faster than light.

But then, something unexpected happened. AST-5O4 avoided the attack, and before Aaradhy could finish his sentence, BOOM! Atharv created an alternative universe and caused a big bang inside it. However, it had no effect on AST-5O4.

Suddenly, a voice came out of AST-5O4, “Ho ho ho ho! Now it’s my turn to attack!” They were all teleported to the void in the middle of space and time, and suddenly, tick!

Aaradhy and Atharv found themselves on the brink of death. Suddenly, Atharv glitches back into his dimension on Earth, but Aaradhy remained trapped in the void with AST-5O4. The devil threatened to destroy every dimension, every single string.

Aaradhy spoke, struggling to catch his breath, “No, no, no! You can destroy me, but not my dimensions”

Suddenly, there was a loud, piercing noise, and everything went silent.

Suddenly, Aaradhy was dead, a tragic but true end to his story. AST-5O4 began to rule every universe, and Aaradhy's body was locked inside a box made of TRAZMACRANIUMFURTCHAZTRA, the world's strongest material, worth over 5 million T+ USD $.

One day, Atharv secretly approached the box and used a special method to vibrate the strings of the universe, allowing him to change the material and take his brother's body out of the box. The A/A's gang was now just the A Gang. If anyone found out what Atharv had done, they would be in grave danger.

After 10 years of hard work, Atharv finally completed the machine. It had the power to bring the dead back to life using Aaradhy's DNA, but he made it solely for his brother to use. The machine was a plasma invisible suit, and when Aaradhy was brought back to life, he spoke in a soft voice, rapidly breathing and asking "FOSTAVU?" Atharv didn't understand what he meant until he realized that when a person doesn't breathe, walk, drink, eat or move their body, they tend to forget everything. So he programmed the invisible plasma suit to react to the air's frequency and move Aaradhy's body parts.

Aaradhy then spent a month learning how to walk again and underwent painful surgeries to learn how to talk, which involved matching his genes, DNA, heartbeats, and Atharv's brain and connecting it to all the memories he had in advanced technology.

After finally remembering everything, Aaradhy expressed his gratitude to his brother, saying, "OMG, Thank you so much for bringing me back to life! I don't know how I can ever repay you."

Atharv replied in a gentle and kind voice, "It's fine, just making sure you owe me one."

Aaradhy replied with enthusiasm, "SURE!!!!!!!"

As they continued to plan, Aaradhy and Atharv realized that changing every single light source was not feasible. Instead, they came up with a new plan to insert radioactive signals into the AST-5O4 robot. They worked tirelessly to implement the plan and eventually succeeded.

As they approached the AST_5O4, they saw that it was heavily guarded by the AI robots. Atharv activated the dison spear, and it emitted a powerful energy beam towards the AST_5O4, destroying some of the AI robots in the process.

AST_5O4 was surprised and angry to see Aaradhy alive. It spoke, "What? How are you alive? Well, I guess I will have fun killing you two times, including your brother."

"Not today," Aaradhy and Atharv said simultaneously with determination in their voices.

Aaradhy tackled the AST_5O4 while it was trying to grab him in its hand. The AST_5O4 fell down, and now it only had access to three dimensions again. Aaradhy was glad that this happened because now it was a fair and square match. As a result, the AST_5O4 could only move in four directions: back, forward, down, and jump. It had no control over time as it was limited to the 3rd dimension.

As Atharv and Aaradhy were on the back of the AST_5O4, they realized that they could use its power source to create a sort of white hole that would spit out objects. They quickly got to work, modifying the AST_5O4's systems to redirect its energy and create a portal. It wasn't easy, but after a few tense moments, the portal opened up and began spitting out the AST_5O4's own energy. Aaradhy and Atharv were successful this time! They had defeated the AST_5O4 and saved their world.

With the AST-5O4 defeated, Aaradhy and Atharv were hailed as heroes across the multiverse. They had saved countless lives and brought peace to the many worlds that had been threatened by the robot's destructive power. Aaradhy and Atharv returned home, proud of their accomplishment and ready for their next adventure.

In Search of Diamond

WRITTEN BY

NAVYA VIDYARTHI

CLASS – 4

DELHI PUBLIC SCHOOL, BOPAL
AHMEDABAD, GUJARAT

27

IN SEARCH OF DIAMOND

"The impossible exists only until we find a way to make it possible"

– Mike Horn

"What is this shining stone, Mom?" I asked to my mother with great excitement. "This is a diamond necklace, my dear," Mom replied.

"Wow! It's so beautiful. Can I try it on?" I asked eagerly.

"No, dear. You are just 8 years old. This is not a toy or a costume jewellery. It's an expensive piece, and we must handle it with extra care," Mom explained.

I left my mother's room, but her words lingered in my mind, making me restless. To distract myself, I started doing my homework and later went to bed. As part of my routine, I picked up my monthly magazine, "Robin Age," and started reading it. As I flipped through the pages, I stumbled upon an article about a "diamond rain" on Uranus. I was fascinated and read it with great curiosity. Intrigued by the possibility of acquiring as many diamonds as I wanted, I became fixated on the idea of traveling to the planet. After researching and constructing a powerful spaceship (U1A) during my summer vacation, I embarked on an adventurous journey with my little trusty Barbie doll (Baria) by my side.

On the way to Uranus, we passed by the red planet of Mars, its surface was burning like fire. Although we were scared at first, we soon realized that it was just a neighbouring planet. We pressed on, eager to reach our final destination.

In the evening, our journey led us to a massive mountain surrounded by many small objects like moon dancing around it. Intrigued by the sight, we decided to pay the place a visit. As night descended, we found ourselves growing increasingly cold and hungry. Thankfully, we had come prepared and had packed warm clothes and food in our bags. We took a break at the "Mainland Jupiter" restaurant, where we enjoyed a meal while watching the objects dancing around us.

The following morning, we resumed our journey when suddenly Baria spotted rocks and stones being thrown at us. It seemed as though a devil was attacking us. I recalled my mother's advice to worship Shani Dev on Saturdays to appease him and receive his blessings. It was evident to me that this was the consequence of angering Shani Dev.

Not wanting any more misfortune on our journey, we reached into our bag and retrieved some mustard oil. We offered it to Shani Dev, folding our hands with closed eyes and wishing to be in his good books always.

Finally, we arrived at our destination. Our mission was clear: to search for diamonds.

We walked for a while and then we saw something glittering in the distance. We ran towards it and found a cave full of sparkling diamonds.

We couldn't believe our eyes. We had struck gold, or rather diamonds. We started collecting as many diamonds as we could fit in our bags. It was hard work, but it was worth it. After a while, we had collected enough diamonds to fill our spaceship. We were over the moon, or over Uranus rather.

But suddenly, we heard a loud noise coming from outside the cave. We looked outside and saw a group of aliens approaching us. They looked friendly, but we were still scared. They greeted us and asked us what we were doing on Uranus. We told them about our mission to collect diamonds, and they laughed.

They told us that they had been collecting diamonds from Uranus for centuries, and they had a much more efficient way of doing it. They showed us their technology and it was amazing. They had machines that could extract diamonds from the ground without having to do it manually.

They offered to help us and we accepted. They showed us how to use their machines and we were able to collect even more diamonds in a fraction of the time it had taken us before. We were grateful to the aliens and thanked them for their help.

After spending few days on Uranus, we planned to returned back to home. We set on our journey with full of memories and said bye to our new friends. We were too much excited to show diamonds which we collected to our family and friends. It was an exciting and unforgettable trip.

***

A
GOOD CORONA
WRITTEN BY
HEENA SETIA
EX. SCIENTIST/ENGINEER
SPACE APPLICATIONS CENTRE
ISRO, AHMEDABAD, GUJARAT
© Team Velocity

28

A GOOD CORONA

"We are not living in fear. We are living in faith."

– CaringBridge

Everything was going smoothly until one day, a college notice shattered all of our dreams. We were sent home for an uncertain period of time, all because of COVID-19. This was a new word to us and we soon learned that it was one of the most dangerous diseases that we would have to face.

Numerous news channels were airing the critical situation of the patients. We were all at home, watching the scary scenes and the numerous cries of people. It was a disaster for us. The government had announced a lockdown, and we were all confined to our houses, watching the news channels. It was at this time that humans realized how animals are treated. We felt trapped, as though we were living in a prison called home.

Prayers and hope were the only things we could hold onto during those trying times. We were all losing our loved ones, which left us feeling emotionally and mentally drained. All we could do was hope for a cure, a medicine that could cure the deadly COVID-19 disease.

It is often said that we should try and try until we succeed, and that is exactly what our doctors and scientists did. We were fortunate to have access to amazing medical facilities, and most importantly, the staff who worked tirelessly to find a cure for the COVID-19 disease. Their perseverance and dedication paid off, as they succeeded in developing vaccines and treatments that helped control the spread of the virus. One fine day, a little smile returned to our faces when we heard the news about COVID-19 vaccinations.

We were all overjoyed, and it was clear that we needed to get vaccinated to protect ourselves and others. However, rumors and misinformation spread, causing some to doubt the safety and efficacy of the vaccine. Despite this, many people stepped forward to get vaccinated and proved the rumors wrong. With more and more people getting vaccinated, we could finally see a light at the end of the tunnel and hope for a better tomorrow.

❧

As everyone was getting vaccinated, I too went to receive my dose. The vaccination requires two initial doses followed by a booster dose. I have already received my two initial doses and returned to the hospital a month later for my booster dose.

I sat in front of the nurse, and she proceeded to administer my booster dose. However, in the middle of the process, she received a phone call and began discussing the number of patients in the hospital.

During the conversation, the syringe containing my vaccine dose remained in her hand, but it was empty. After a two-minute conversation, she approached me and unwittingly administered the dose again. Not realizing the mistake, I assumed this was part of the procedure and remained silent.

That day after receiving the booster dose, I felt extremely uncomfortable, as if something unusual was happening inside my body. I was extremely worried, and thoughts about the dose kept running through my mind. Later, after dinner, while lying in bed, I still felt very unstable. My inner voice kept telling me that I had received an overdose, which caused me to feel stressed and afraid. I felt as though this could be my last day. Eventually, I fell asleep while still contemplating my situation.

ꕥ

The next morning, I slowly opened my eyes and realized that everything around me was blurry. As I sat in the balcony, sipping on a cup of tea, I noticed my neighbor aunty, who had contracted COVID-19, sitting on a chair. Beside her, I saw something unusual- a green-colored, unstable, unshaped particle that seemed to be fighting against the good bacteria in her body. I was shocked by what I was seeing.

As a result of an overdose, my mind started to think about the possibility of being able to see the coronavirus with my naked eyes, and I wondered if I was the only one who could see them. Hours later, I went to the market to buy groceries and put on a mask for protection against the virus. As I looked around, I saw many people surrounded by green-colored particles, which I assumed were the coronavirus. It was one of the scariest scenes I had ever witnessed. In a moment of panic, I shouted, "Please leave!" Suddenly, the green particles turned and looked at me, and one of them asked, "Who are you and how can you see us?" Fearing for my safety, I ran out of the market and back to my home, where I hid under my bed.

After spending 15 minutes under my bed, the haunting scenes of people screaming due to the coronavirus replayed in my mind. It was clear that we were all in danger. As I believed I could see the virus, I thought that perhaps I could also communicate with it and find a solution to this problem. I began researching the origins of the virus, tracing it back to a city in China.

❧

After two days, I purchased tickets and made my way to China, feeling both curious and fearful about facing the coronavirus army. Upon arrival, I started walking and talking to myself, wondering where I could find this dangerous virus.

As I walked for a few miles, I found myself in a large fish market where I could see a lot of green particles, which I knew were the coronavirus. It was a surreal experience because I was the only one who could see them. I managed to make my way to a nearby building and sat on the stairs, pondering a solution. As I observed the particles, I noticed some red-colored particles fighting against the green ones. The red particles were few in number, and despite their valiant efforts to protect people, they were no match for the powerful green particles. One of the red particles was hiding near me, and I was able to see him clearly. When I started guiding him, he was shocked that I can see him and talk with him. I then told everything about me and spoke with him and learned about the situation, how the green particles were attacking the human body, killing immunity and attacking multiple times.

After speaking with the red particle, I realized the danger posed by the green particles and began to formulate a plan with the red particle. I allowed the red particle to enter my body and help me become two times stronger to fight against the green particles.

As I fought alongside the red particle, I felt like a superhero on a mission to save humanity from the dangerous virus. Together, we worked tirelessly and managed to create an anti-virus within a few hours. With our anti-virus, we were able to kill all of the green particles, leaving only the red ones behind. It was a victorious moment, and I was grateful for the red particle's help in defeating the dangerous coronavirus.

There is a saying that bad things or negative energy don't last forever because goodness and positivity are immortal. It seemed to hold true as the good Corona (the red particle) helped me win the battle against the dangerous green Corona (coronavirus). It was a testament to the power of positivity and the resilience of the human spirit in the face of adversity.

***

Connecting
the
Dots
WRITTEN BY
Sushil Kumar
ASST. MANAGER
UNION BANK OF INDIA
SAHARANPUR, UTTAR PRADESH
© Team Velocity

29

CONNECTING THE DOTS

"When you look at the stars and the galaxy, you feel that you are not just from any particular piece of land, but from the solar system."

– Kalpana Chawla

Once upon a time, there was a young boy named Rohan who lived in a small village in India. Rohan studied in a government school, and he had a deep curiosity about the world around him. One of his favorite things was to lie down in the open field near his house and gaze up at the night sky.

He would spend hours connecting the stars, imagining them as different shapes and patterns, just like the dot-to-dot pictures in his school books. He loved tracing imaginary lines between the stars, creating his own constellations and stories. Rohan was particularly fascinated by a group of seven stars that he often saw arranged in the shape of a dipper. Out of these seven starts, 3 stars were in the slant line and 4 stars in the square.

Rohan was curious to learn more about these seven stars above him and began to read books about astronomy. He wanted to understand the mysteries of the universe and the stories behind the constellations of these seven stars that he saw every night. He was amazed by the beauty and complexity of the stars above, and he felt a sense of wonder and awe every time he looked up at the night sky.

One day Rohan asked his grandfather about the constellation of these seven stars. His grandfather told him, "It was called the Saptarishi constellation and that it held great significance in Hindu mythology. The term 'Saptarishi' is taken from the Sanskrit word 'Saptarshi' which literally translated as 'Seven Sages' or 'Seven Rishis' who are admired at many places in the Vedas and other Hindu literature. In ancient Indian astronomy, the asterism of the Big Dipper (part of the constellation of Ursa Major) is called Saptarshi Mandala, with the seven stars of the Saptarshi Mandala representing seven rishis, namely "Vashistha", "Marichi", "Pulastya", "Pulaha", "Atri", "Angiras" and "Kratu".

His gradfather further told, "Contrary to popular belief, there are eight stars, not seven stars in the Saptarishi constellation. There is a binary star system in this constellation – made of two stars rotating around each other. In western astronomy, they are known as Alcor and Mizar, while in India, they are called Arundhati and Vashishth."

His Grandfather added that it is also believed that The Saptarishis (seven sages) are the seven mind born sons of Brahma. They live for a period of time known as a manvantar (306,720,000 Earth Years). During this period of time they serve as representatives of Brahma. At the end of a manvantara the universe gets destroyed. The "Saptarishi" keeps changing for every Manvantara.

Rohan was surprised to know about the mysteries of these stars and their relation with the Indian mythology.

As Rohan grew older, he never lost his fascination for the night sky. Even when he went away to college, he would still sneak out at night to look up at the stars. He would still connect the dots, still make up stories in his head, still marvel at the vastness and mystery of the universe. He continued to stargaze every chance he got, and his love for astronomy eventually led him to pursue a career in the field.

Many years later, Rohan's dream came true. He was selected to be part of a team of scientists and astronauts on a mission to explore a distant planet. The team has discovered a strange planet orbiting a star in the Saptarishi constellation. This strange planet had an unusual atmosphere and was home to a diverse ecosystem of alien creatures.

Rohan was a skilled and dedicated scientist, with a passion for understanding the mysteries of the universe. He had worked tirelessly to prepare for this mission, studying the planet's environment, analyzing data from previous space missions, and developing new tools and techniques to help the team better understand the alien ecosystem they were about to explore.

Along with the team of scientists and astronauts, Rohan settled into a spaceship, which was specially designed for long-term space travel. They rechecked their equipment, ran through emergency procedures, and went over their mission objectives one more time. With a sense of anticipation, the spaceship began to move, accelerating steadily as it left Earth's atmosphere and headed out into the vast expanse of space. Rohan felt a sense of excitement and anticipation unlike anything he had experienced before. This was the culmination of a dream he had nurtured since childhood, and he was determined to make the most of this opportunity.

As they traveled farther and farther from home, the team watched the stars and galaxies pass by, feeling a sense of wonder and awe at the enormity of the universe. As Rohan looked out the window of the spacecraft, he saw the stars he had loved so much all his life, now closer than ever before.

Throughout the journey, Rohan was a key member of the team, working closely with his fellow scientists and astronauts to solve problems, analyze data, and push the boundaries of human knowledge. He approached each new challenge with a combination of intellectual curiosity and practical ingenuity, always seeking new insights and understanding.

Days turned into weeks, and weeks turned into months as the ship traveled through the void of space. The team worked diligently, conducting experiments, analyzing data, and preparing for the challenges that lay ahead.

As the team landed on the strange planet, Rohan felt a sense of wonder and awe at the diversity of life that surrounded him. He was surprised to see that they were greeted by a group of seven humanoid beings, each with unique characteristics and abilities. Rohan was amazed to discover that these beings were the Saptarishis, the legendary sages of Hindu mythology.

The Saptarishis introduced themselves as Vashistha, Marichi, Pulastya, Pulaha, Atri, Angiras, and Kratu. Each of them possessed incredible knowledge and wisdom, and they were eager to share it with the explorers.

Rohan spent months on the planet along with team of scientists and astronauts, learning from the Saptarishis and studying the planet's unique ecosystem. He spent long hours exploring the alien ecosystem, studying the behavior of the strange creatures that lived there, and conducting experiments to better understand the planet's environment. He discovered that the Saptarishis had created a perfect balance of life on the planet, with each creature playing a vital role in the ecosystem.

Rohan soon realized that the planet was in danger. A massive asteroid was hurtling towards the planet, threatening to destroy everything in its path.

The Saptarishis were calm in the face of this danger. They knew that they could not stop the asteroid, but they could prepare for its impact. They taught Rohan how to build a shield to protect the planet from the asteroid's impact.

Working together, Rohan and the Saptarishis built the shield and prepared for the asteroid's impact. When it finally struck, the shield held, and the planet was saved.

Rohan was amazed by the knowledge and wisdom of the Saptarishis. They realized that these beings were not just legends, but real entities with incredible power and intelligence.

As Rohan left the planet, he promised to share his knowledge of the Saptarishis with the rest of the galaxy. He knew that this discovery would change the way he viewed the universe, and he was excited to see what the future held for humanity. Rohan felt a sense of deep satisfaction, knowing that he had played a crucial role in one of the greatest scientific expeditions of all time.

"The stars, planets, and galaxies above us have always fascinated humankind. Our journey to understand them is a journey to understand ourselves and the universe."

– Dr. A. P. J. Abdul Kalam

A NEW DIMENSION

WRITTEN BY
SUMIT KUMAR
SCIENTIST/ENGINEER
SPACE APPLICATIONS CENTRE
ISRO, AHMEDABAD, GUJARAT

30

A NEW DIMENSION

"Science is a way of thinking much more than it is a body of knowledge."

– Carl Sagan

In the celestial realm of heaven, the two great minds once again found themselves in each other's company. Sir Isaac Newton and Albert Einstein found themselves in the afterlife, standing on a fluffy white cloud in front of the pearly gates of heaven.

Einstein was feeling very hungry and decided to explore the surrounding area in search of food. As he roamed through space, he stumbled upon an apple tree and was surprised to see it heavily laden with apples. He approached the tree and plucked an apple, then noticed a nearby bench where he sat down to eat. After taking the first bite, he marvelled at the sweetness of the fruit and tossed the core behind him, but he didn't hear it hit the ground. He felt as if someone had caught the apple, preventing it from falling.

Suddenly, he heard a voice from behind him. Turning around, he saw someone holding the apple he had just thrown. The person explained that the apples in this location were especially sweet because there was no gravity.

Einstein stood up quickly and turned around. To his surprise, he found someone holding the apple he had just thrown. As their eyes met, they exchanged a knowing nod of recognition.

"Goodness gracious me!" exclaimed Einstein, his eyes wide open. "Newton, is that really you? What are you doing here?"

Newton chuckled. "I could ask you the same question, my friend. It seems that our contributions to science have earned us a place here in the great beyond, in this new dimension."

Einstein asked Newton in surprise, "But you look exactly the same as we saw in your pictures on earth. How is that possible?"

Newton chuckled and quipped, "Did you forget my first law of motion? An object at rest stays at rest unless acted upon by an external force. Since there's no force here in space, I've remained the same."

After Newton's witty remark, they both burst into laughter, enjoying each other's company and the humor of the situation. The two scientists fell into an animated discussion about the mysteries of the universe. They compared notes on their greatest discoveries, debated various theories, and even shared a few jokes.

As they talked, they suddenly realized they had a problem. While they could understand each other perfectly well, they were speaking different languages! Newton was speaking in 17th-century English, and Einstein was speaking in 20th-century German.

"How can we understand each other?" Newton asked.

Einstein scratched his head thoughtfully. "Perhaps we need a new theory of relativity. One that transcends time and space."

Newton raised an eyebrow. "And how exactly do you propose we do that?"

Einstein grinned. "Well, I have an idea. Let's create a new language. We'll call it Newteinian."

Newton chuckled. "Newteinian? That sounds ridiculous!"

Einstein replied, "Well, it's either that or we'll have to learn each other's languages. And I don't know about you, but my 17th-century English is a little rusty."

The two scientists put their heads together and came up with a new language that combined elements of English and German, creating a unique blend that allowed them to understand each other perfectly.

As they continued their conversation, they discussed the nature of the afterlife, the origins of the universe, and even the possibility of time travel.

Newton: "Einstein, Your theories of relativity revolutionized the field of physics."

Einstein: "Thank you, but it was your work on classical mechanics that paved the way for my discoveries."

Newton: "Yes, it's amazing how our contributions to science have impacted the world."

Einstein: "Indeed, I often wonder what new discoveries we could have made if we had collaborated together during our lifetimes."

Newton: "It's an interesting thought, but perhaps we were meant to make our own individual contributions to science."

Einstein: "Perhaps you're right. But I'm still curious about your thoughts on the nature of gravity."

Newton: "Ah, yes. I believe that gravity is a force that attracts objects to one another in proportion to their masses."

Einstein: "Fascinating. My theory of general relativity describes gravity as the curvature of space-time caused by mass and energy."

Newton: "It's amazing how our different theories complement each other. Together, we have advanced our understanding of the universe."

Einstein: "Yes, and I believe that our work will continue to inspire future generations of scientists to explore the mysteries of the cosmos."

As they delved deeper into their discussion, the celestial surroundings seemed to shimmer with a renewed sense of wonder. The stars twinkled brighter, as if they, too, were captivated by the exchange of ideas between these intellectual giants.

Newton, with a playful glint in his eye, leaned closer to Einstein. "You know, Albert, I sometimes wonder what would have happened if we had collaborated on a grand unified theory of physics."

Einstein chuckled. "Ah, the union of Newtonian mechanics and the theory of relativity. It would have been a formidable endeavor. But who knows, perhaps our celestial reunion is a chance to explore such possibilities."

As their minds brimmed with excitement over the possibilities of a collaborative grand unified theory, Newton's mischievous grin grew wider. "Albert, my dear friend, I have a surprise for you. Come, follow me," he beckoned, gesturing toward a distant cloud.

Intrigued, Einstein followed Newton through the celestial expanse. As they approached the cloud, it transformed into a magnificent golden archway leading to a grand hall. The archway sparkled with the names of the greatest scientific minds that had come before them, carved into the ethereal material.

Newton turned to Einstein with a twinkle in his eye. "Welcome to the Hall of Luminary Minds, a place where the spirits of brilliant scientists gather to celebrate their contributions to the world of science."

Einstein's eyes widened with awe as he stepped through the archway and into the hall. The air was filled with the hum of animated discussions, and he could hear snippets of conversations about quantum mechanics, cosmology, genetics, and so much more.

They walked further into the hall, passing luminous figures engrossed in passionate debates. Einstein's gaze fell upon a group of scientists discussing the intricacies of quantum entanglement, while nearby, others were unraveling the mysteries of black holes.

Newton leaned over and whispered, "Here, time and space converge, allowing great minds from different eras to interact and exchange ideas."

Einstein's heart swelled with joy as he realized that the spirits of those who had come before him were not lost to the annals of history but lived on in this ethereal gathering. The hall was filled with renowned scientists like Galileo, Kepler, Marie Curie, and countless others, their luminous forms engaged in intellectual discourse.

Newton guided Einstein toward a cluster of scientists engaged in a lively discussion about the fundamental nature of the universe. Among them, Einstein spotted his old mentor, Max Planck, and the enigmatic quantum theorist, Niels Bohr.

Einstein approached them with an eager smile. "Max, Niels, it's an honor to be in your presence. I've longed to discuss my ideas on quantum mechanics with you."

Planck, a kind smile gracing his ethereal form, welcomed Einstein warmly. "Albert, we have eagerly awaited your arrival. Your theory of relativity brought forth a new era of scientific understanding."

Bohr, his eyes sparkling with curiosity, added, "Indeed, Albert. Your insights have pushed the boundaries of our understanding and opened doors to new realms of possibility."

Einstein felt a surge of gratitude and humility. To be acknowledged and embraced by the scientific giants who had laid the foundation for his own work was an indescribable honor.

As the discussions in the hall continued, Einstein found himself immersed in conversations with scientists from various disciplines, exchanging ideas, challenging assumptions, and reveling in the sheer joy of intellectual exploration. The symphony of scientific discourse echoed through the hall, weaving together the knowledge of past and present, transcending the limitations of time and space.

Newton, observing Einstein's enthusiasm, smiled with satisfaction. "This, Albert, is the essence of science—continual growth, collaboration, and the pursuit of truth. Here, in the Hall of Luminary Minds, we stand united by our shared passion for unravelling the mysteries of the universe."

Einstein nodded, his eyes shining with newfound inspiration. "Newton, my friend, you have shown me a treasure beyond measure. I am grateful for this celestial reunion and the opportunity to engage with the greatest minds of all time."

And so, amidst the celestial splendour of the Hall of Luminary Minds, Einstein found himself forever entwined with the luminous spirits of those who had shaped the course of scientific progress.

As their conversation comes to an end, Newton and Einstein reflect on their legacies and how their work will continue to shape science for generations to come. They both feel proud of what they accomplished in life and are grateful for the opportunity to meet each other in heaven.

They both agreed that their work on Earth was not finished yet. They were eager to return to the mortal plane and continue their research.

So, the two great minds bid each other farewell, knowing that they would meet again in the future, perhaps in another dimension or even in another life.

And with that, they both descended from the cloud and disappear into a bright light with eager to continue their quest for knowledge and discovery.

***

COMPETITIONS

ORGANIZED BY

TEAM VELOCITY

ESSAY WRITING COMPETITION-2020

During the Covid-19 pandemic, children's education was among the most severely impacted areas worldwide. In response, Team Velocity organized an online essay writing competition in the year 2020 aimed at helping children stay connected with their studies. The competition focused on the theme "***The Impact of COVID-19 on the Education System of India***" and attracted 243 participants of Class-6 to Class-12 from across the country. Winners of the competition were recognized with prizes and certificates, in recognition of their outstanding contributions.

Certainly! Conducting an essay competition during the pandemic was no easy feat, as the entire world was facing unprecedented challenges. However, Team Velocity recognized the importance of education in these difficult times, and came up with a unique solution to keep students engaged and motivated. By leveraging technology, the competition was able to reach children from all corners of the country, despite the restrictions imposed by the pandemic. This not only helped children continue their studies, but also provided a platform for them to express their thoughts and opinions on the impact of Covid-19 on their education. Overall, the competition was a great success and provided a ray of hope for students and educators alike during these trying times.

SPACE QUIZ COMPETITION-2021

Team Velocity organized an exciting Online Space Quiz Competition in the year 2021 for the students from Class-3 to Class-8. The competition aimed to promote scientific learning and create interest in the field of space exploration. The quiz consisted of multiple choice questions related to space science, astronomy, and space exploration.

The competition was held entirely online, allowing students from across the country to participate without any geographical constraints. This not only made the competition more accessible but also added an element of excitement as students were able to compete with their peers from different regions.

Over 500 students participated in the competition, showcasing their knowledge and passion for space science. The top-performing students were awarded with exciting prizes and certificates of recognition.

The Online Space Quiz Competition-2021 was not only a fun-filled activity for students, but it also helped to ignite a love for space and science among the younger generation. By making learning interactive and engaging, Team Velocity has set a new standard in promoting scientific education in India.

VELOCITY SPACE QUIZ COMPETITION-2021
SATVIKA SAINI, CLASS-6 (GROUP-B)
KAMESHWAR EDUCATION CAMPUS
AHMEDABAD, GUJARAT

VELOCITY SPACE QUIZ COMPETITION-2021
SPACE
Space Central School
Aaishwarya Meshram, Class 4 (Group-A)
K.Nanda kishore, Class 3 (Group A)
Aadarsh Meshram, Class 6 (Group B)
K.Subhiksha, Class 6 (Group-B)
Andhra Pradesh

SCIENCE FICTION STORY WRITING COMPETITION-2022

Team VELOCITY invited all participants to showcase their literary prowess to the world by writing their most intriguing science fiction story. It's time to let your imagination run wild and let the ink flow! The best stories will be carefully evaluated and selected for publication, and the winners will receive both a prize and a certificate of recognition. This is an incredible opportunity to share your creative vision with a wider audience and be recognized for your writing skills. So what are you waiting for? Submit your story today and let your voice be heard!

Rules and Guidelines:

Following were the rules and guidelines defined for the students.

- The competition is open for the students of class 5 to class 12 from all the schools and colleges. The student has to provide the school ID card, failing which the story will be treated as invalid entry.
- The candidate has to complete their registration by filling registration form.
- Only 1 story allowed from one student. (no co-author allowed).

- Stories must be no more than 2000 words.
- Stories must be written in either Hindi or English on Science fact/fiction.
- The story must be original and it should not be published anywhere.
- All entries are final. No revisions are accepted.
- The stories must be accepted only in hand-written format (scanned. pdf file).
- The student should submit his story in the given format. Each entry must have a cover page, which will include Competition Name, title of the story, the author's details (name, class and School name, address, telephone number and email address). Every subsequent page must include the title of the story at the top of each page and page number at bottom, but NOT the author's name.
- All the stories will be evaluated by a panel of experts. The decision of the panel will be final.
- The team velocity reserves the right to edit the story or title of the story, if required during publication.
- Please submit your story on or before the last date.

Evaluation Criteria:

Following were the evaluation criteria followed during evaluation of the stories by the expert panel.

S.No.	Parameters	Detail
1	Story format	Story must be written as per rules and guidelines mentioned for the competition. It mainly include the cover page as well as story name and page number mentioned.
2	Title of the story	The title of the story must be related with the theme of the competition. The best title, which defines your story.
3	Handwriting	It includes the beautiful handwriting, grammatical mistakes and sentence formation.
4	Word length	Story must be limited to 1000-2000 words.
5	Beginning of the story	The beginning of the story, which attracts the reader to read further.
6	Writing style	It includes the story writing style. How much better do you connect the flow of the story and conversation between the characters of the story
7	The plot and characters of the story	It includes the characters you choose for the story as per the title of the story.
8	Imagination	It includes your imagination power that how better you can think of science fiction.
9	Originality	It includes any new idea for science fiction, which is not inspired from any other story or film released earlier. The story must be original and it should not be published anywhere, otherwise it will be rejected outrightly.
10	Story conveying any message	It includes that the story conveying any message for our society or inspiring the people.

Prize and Certificate:

- E-certificate will be provided to all the participants.
- Prize for top-3 stories along with certificate in both the categories – Hindi and English.
- The shortlisted top 25 stories in both the categories (Hindi and English) will be published in the form of book/e-book.

EVALUATION TEAM

All the stories have been evaluated by a team of experts who are highly knowledgeable in the fields of science, literature, language, and writing. The evaluation team includes experienced professionals with extensive experience in their respective fields. They have followed the specified evaluation criteria to ensure their evaluations are accurate, thorough, and unbiased. The team uses a standardized evaluation process to assess each story based on its originality, creativity, coherence, and overall quality. They understand the importance of creativity and imagination in storytelling, and they work hard to ensure that each story is evaluated fairly and accurately. Their evaluations are based on objective criteria and are designed to provide constructive feedback to help authors improve their writing skills.

The members in the evaluation team includes –

Dr. Divya Rajeswari Swaminathan is from Chennai, Tamil Nadu. She has completed her PhD in Geography and Geoinformatics from University of Bonn, Germany. Ms. Divya has worked in both national and international organisations for environmental protection and conservation. She is presently working as Assistant Professor at Banglore University.

Jayashree Jana Bhattacharya belongs to Calcutta, West Bengal. She did her M.Tech from Calcutta University. Presently she is working as Scientist/ Engineer in ISRO, Bangalore. She has also worked as a scientist for 7 years at Satish Dhawan Space Center, ISRO, Sriharikota. She is sports enthusiast and won multiple awards. She is involved in yoga and loves to stay active. She enjoys reading books and exploring new places.

Gulshan Khandelwal belongs to Noida, Uttar Pradesh. She did her B.Tech in Electronics and Communication Engineering from Rajasthan University and M.Tech in Microwave Electronics from University of Delhi. She has worked as a lecturer in engineering college. She has also worked as Microwave Network Planner in DragonWave HFCL for Reliance Jio project. Currently she is actively involved in social activities. She likes travelling and learning new things.

Mahashreveta Choudhary belongs to New Delhi. She did masters in Mass Communication from MCU Bhopal. After working for 2 years in mainstream journalism, She has been writing and curating thought provoking and engaging content for geospatial industry.

Anand Kumar Mishra hails from a small town of Khaga-Fatehpur, Uttar Pradesh. He obtained his bachelor degree from Allahabad University, as well as degrees in law, education, and post-graduation from Kanpur University. He is currently working as a teacher in English Medium Primary School at Malukpur village in the Airayan Block of Fatehpur district, Uttar Pradesh. He has a keen interest in innovative and environmental education, and he enjoy interacting with children. His several research papers and articles have been published to date. His books on a collection of short stories titled "Traasdi" has been published.

Mukesh Kumar Mishra is working as Library Officer in Space Applications Centre, ISRO, Ahmedabad. He did his B.Sc. (PCM) from Allahabad University, Master's degree in Library and Information Science (MLISc)

with Gold Medal from Banaras Hindu University and M.Phil. in Library and Information Science from Sardar Patel University, Anand, Gujarat. Being in and around books always, he always passionate towards reading. Besides, he likes traveling, exploring and knowing different places and culture.

Richeek Mishra has born in Prayag, raised in Ayodhya. He has done his schooling in Army school Faizabad, till graduation in BSc (Bio) from Awadh University. He did his Master of journalism (MJ) from Makhanlal University of Journalism Bhopal. He is currently working as an assistant editor, mainly focus on the articles related Science and Technology.

Sonu Jain is the Assistant Director (Official Language) at ISRO, Department of Space, Government of India, Ahmedabad. He has completed his M.A. in English Literature, Philosophy, and Sanskrit Literature from the University of Rajasthan, Jaipur as well as M.A. in Hindi Literature from Karnataka University, Mysore. He is pursuing his Ph.D. in the Department of Prakrit, Faculty of Languages, Gujarat University. He has presented many papers in various national-level seminars and has been awarded for his articles multiple times.

SOME GLIMPSE OF THE WINNERS OF SCIENCE FICTION STORY WRITING COMPETITION-2022

VELOCITY SCIENCE FICTION
STORY WRITING COMPETITION-2022

EURO INTERNATI
WINNER- BEST STORY AWARD
Congratulations !!!
Akhil Sharma
Euro International School, Gurgaon, Haryana

VELOCITY SCIENCE FICTION
STORY WRITING
COMPETITION-2022
BEST STORY AWARD
Congratulations !!!
Shreenithi Senthil
(Class-7)
Velammal Vidhyashram,
Chennai, Tamil Nadu

VELOCITY SCIENCE FICTION
STORY WRITING
COMPETITION-2022

BEST STORY AWARD
Congratulations !!!
T.G. Mahauva Lakshmi
(Class-9)
LITTLE FLOWER PUBLIC SCHOOL
TIRUNELVELI, TAMILNADU

VELOCITY SCIENCE FICTION
STORY WRITING
COMPETITION-2022
BEST STORY AWARD
Congratulations !!!
Adnan Nadeem Khan (Class-7)
INTERNATIONAL INDIAN SCHOOL
AL-GHUBRA, MUSCAT, OMAN

BEST STORY AWARD
Congratulations !!!
Kabeer Khan (Class-7)
Bal Bhawan School
Bhopal, Madhya Pradesh

VELOCITY SCIENCE FICTION
STORY WRITING COMPETITION-2022

BEST STORY AWARD
Congratulations !!!
Prisha Arora(Class-9)
Delhi Public School, Bopal
Ahmedabad, Gujarat

VELOCITY SCIENCE FICTION
STORY WRITING
COMPETITION-2022

BEST STORY AWARD
Congratulations !!!
Kashish Maurya(Class-7)
MAHARISHI VIDYA MANDIR
RAIPUR,CHHATTISGARH

VELOCITY SCIENCE FICTION
STORY WRITING
COMPETITION-2022

BEST STORY AWARD
Congratulations !!!
N. Haniya Zahraa (Class-9)
LITTLE FLOWER PUBLIC SCHOOL
TIRUNELVELI, TAMILNADU

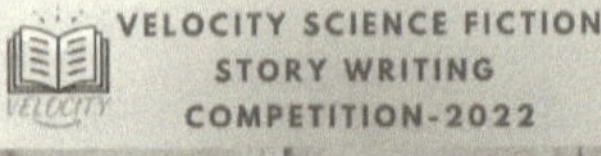

BEST STORY AWARD
Congratulations !!!
Khushboo Kannaujiya
(Class-12)
GURU NANAK ENGLISH MEDIUM SCHOOL
VARANASI, UTTAR PRADESH

BEST STORY AWARD
Congratulations !!!
Harsh Narayan Sharma(Class-11)
St. Mary's School
Khaga-Fatehpur, U.P.

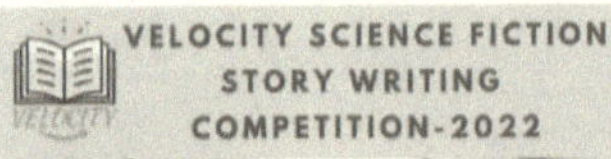

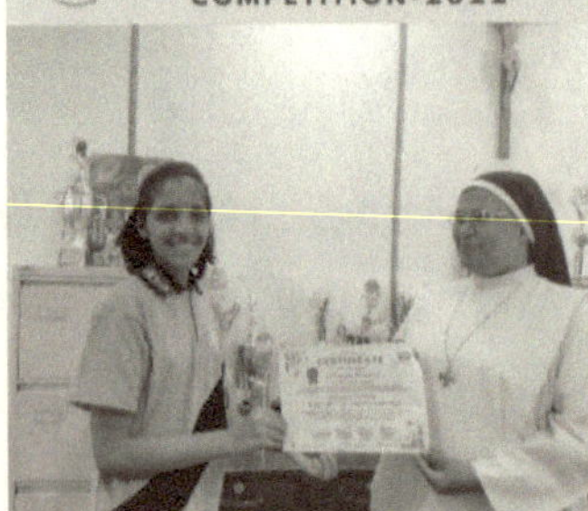

BEST STORY AWARD
Congratulations !!!
Aadya Tiwari (Class-6)
CARMEL CONVENT SENIOR SR. SCHOOL
BHOPAL ,MADHYA PRADESH

BEST STORY AWARD
Congratulations !!!
Aarushi Chouksey (Class-6)
CARMEL CONVENT SENIOR SR. SCHOOL
BHOPAL ,MADHYA PRADESH

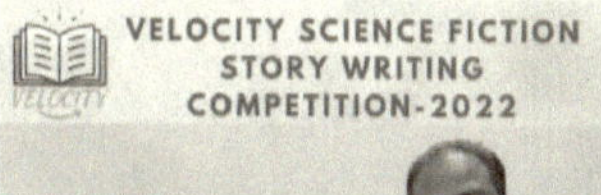

BEST STORY AWARD
Congratulations !!!
Sonal Prajapati (Class-10)
St.Mary's Con. Inter College
Lucknow, Uttar Pradesh

BEST STORY AWARD
Congratulations !!!
ABHINAV BAJPAI
(Class-8)
RVS INTERNATIONAL SCHOOL
FATEHPUR, UTTAR PRADESH

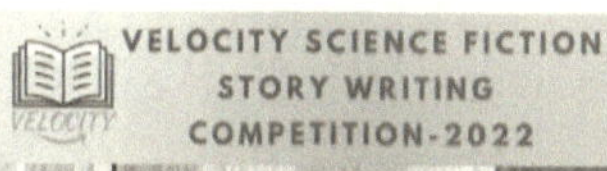

BEST STORY AWARD
Congratulations !!!
SHASHWAT BAJPAI
(Class-8)
RVS INTERNATIONAL SCHOOL
FATEHPUR, UTTAR PRADESH

BEST STORY AWARD
Congratulations !!!
Ayman Nadeem Khan (Class-5)
INTERNATIONAL INDIAN SCHOOL
AL-GHUBRA, MUSCAT, OMAN

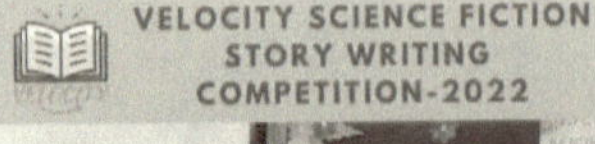

BEST STORY AWARD
Congratulations !!!
Apoorva (Class-7)
KENDRIYA VIDYALAYA
PUNE, MAHARASHTRA

VELOCITY SCIENCE FICTION
STORY WRITING
COMPETITION-2022

BEST STORY AWARD
Congratulations !!!
YUDHVIR SINGH (Class-7)
INDO AMERICAN PUBLIC SCHOOL
UDAIPUR, RAJASTHAN

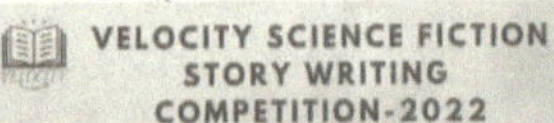

BEST STORY AWARD
Congratulations !!!
Jayanti Gautam
Govt. Polytechnic, Manikpur
Chitrakoot, Uttar Pradesh

VELOCITY SCIENCE FICTION
STORY WRITING
COMPETITION-2022

BEST STORY AWARD
Congratulations !!!
Aadarsh Deepak Meshram (Class-7)
SPACE CENTRAL SCHOOL
NELLORE, ANDHRA PRADESH

"The Story of Young Minds" is an exciting collection of science fiction stories that will take you on a journey through time and space. Explore the depths of the universe, travel through time, and discover new worlds with these imaginative and thought-provoking tales. This book offers a thrilling ride to a new world of imagination. Meet characters who grapple with the consequences of technology, explore the mysteries of the universe, and confront the ethical dilemmas of scientific progress. From aliens to robots, and dystopian societies to the far reaches of outer space, these stories will surely captivate readers of all ages. The authors have crafted each story with care, weaving together complex themes with engaging characters and unexpected plot twists. Each story is crafted to inspire young minds and ignite a love for science fiction. The Story of Young Minds showcases the limitless potential of young writers and is a must-read for anyone who loves science fiction. Join these budding authors on their journey to the stars and beyond.

Do you also have questions in your mind on seeing things that why is it like this? And then you start weaving a story in your mind that what if this happens?

This book is a compilation of such stories from the imaginary world of science generated in the minds of children.

www.ingramcontent.com/pod-product-compliance
Lightning Source LLC
LaVergne TN
LVHW091257150826
845673LV00006B/1447

* 9 7 9 8 8 9 0 2 6 9 6 1 4 *